PRAISE FOR MARGIE BENEDICT

INVADER
"Fans of sci-fi mysteries and strong female characters should snap up this psychological page-turner."
—*Publishers Weekly*

LAST GIRL STANDING
Fast-paced, entertaining, and exciting, with a fresh, believable voice." —*Kirkus Reviews*

THE THIEVES OF MAGIC
Benedict's "prose is crisp and purposeful, charged with feeling, and always attuned to what will engage readers in each moment." —*The BookLife Prize*

"For those who enjoyed Harry Potter but who seek a feisty, determined female protagonist..." —*Midwest Book Review*

"A gripping fantasy adventure. A BRONZE MEDAL WINNER and highly recommended."
—*The Wishing Shelf Book Awards*

Silver Medalist, 2018 SPR Book Awards: "A stellar entry into the genre of YA fantasy."

BEFORE SHE WAS TAKEN
"This was such an amazing novel to read... The characters were wonderfully written... This novel was a fast read for me and I greatly recommend it.." —*Bookshelf Adventures*

THE TRIALS

ORIGINAL GODS
BOOK 1

MARGIE BENEDICT

For Gordon,
Thank you for all your support!
Love,
Margie Benedict

FIRST EDITION, DECEMBER 2024

Copyright © 2024 by Marjory Benedict
All rights reserved. This book or any portion thereof may not be reproduced or used in any manner whatsoever without the express written permission of the publisher except for the use of brief quotations in a book review.

This is a work of fiction. Names, characters, businesses, places, events, and incidents are either the products of the author's imagination or used in a fictitious manner. Any resemblance to actual persons, living or dead, or actual events is purely coincidental.

Publisher: margiebenedict.com
Cover Design: ebooklaunch.com

ISBN: 978-1-954584-47-1 (ebook)
ISBN: 978-1-954584-48-8 (paperback)

Printed in the United States of America

PART I

DISSENT

In the beginning, immortals closely watched over the lives of mortals. Later, desiring that their children learn self-reliance, the immortals chose not to walk among them for thousands of years. This period came to be known as the Dark Age.

During the Dark Age, the race of mortals gradually weakened until they brought a pestilence upon themselves. This was the Great Scourge.

Afterward, the immortals returned to guide the few surviving mortals back to a place of strength and enlightenment. This is the Golden Age.

- The Book of Immortals

1

I, ASTERIOS

Sometimes I had disloyal thoughts, particularly when Moros struck me with his riding crop.

I didn't know what his problem was, but he was lashing me more often lately. If I had a forgiving nature, I would brush it off. But I did not have a forgiving nature. I had a long memory that held a notch for each wrong enacted against me. I was sixty-nine years old, and that represented a lot of notches, even for a blest horse.

"Slow down," Moros said. "Henry can't keep up."

The immortal was riding on my back, while Henry—whose real name was Belic—walked alongside. He actually could keep up, but chose not to. He preferred to hang back to keep Moros from noticing his attention straying while the immortal lectured him.

It was difficult for me to walk any slower. I was, of course, larger than a regular horse—taller and more regal and designed for galloping across emerald plains beneath azure skies. The blest horses' most significant distinction, though, was intelligence. In that regard, we were like mortals compared to apes of the forest.

Moros had never been one to allow me to gallop unless he had an urgent need. These days I was not even permitted a gentle trot.

"How are your studies going, Henry?" Moros asked.

In the last few months, Belic had grown accustomed to the immortal calling him Henry and asking him about his studies.

"Very good, sir," Belic said. Moros had encouraged him to address him as *sir*, although it was customary to call the immortals *my lord* or *my lady*. "My tutor says I'm the best he ever taught in math."

I doubted whether the boy could add two plus two. He was a seventeen-year-old defender chosen to undergo the Trials a year ago, and had somehow survived. His studies consisted of lessons in sword-fighting and archery, not math and literature, as Moros seemed to imagine. Luckily for him, the immortal never quizzed him.

"I'm glad to hear it," Moros said. "And physics? It's essential to have a strong understanding of science these days."

Is it? I wondered. I was not sure what physics was, but I had never observed a mortal speaking of science as if they understood the subject either.

"My physics tutor says it's like a miracle how quick I learn everything."

I snort, confident that neither of them would recognize it for the laugh that it was.

"You make me proud, Henry. Keep up the good work," Moros said.

"Yes, sir." Meanwhile the boy's eyes strayed across the path to where a silver coin glittered on the grass. Someone must have dropped it. Moros must've glimpsed it too, because he said, "Fetch the coin, Henry. Give it to my assistant when we get back."

The boy wasted no time in retrieving it. "I will, sir. You can count on me."

I held back another snort. Belic would keep that coin for himself. I'd observed him frequently pilfering items of value from Moros. Once it was a small silver flask; another time, a gold clasp that came loose from the immortal's tunic. The boy was quite light-fingered when it came to snatching things up. I had seen him eyeing the slender gold medallion that hung around Moros's neck and sometimes fell into view, but it would be a challenge for even Belic to remove it without the immortal noticing. I knew from past observation that the object was of particular significance.

The boy helped Moros to dismount when we reached the lookout. They stood together staring out toward the settlements. Mostly the trees blocked sight of the distant buildings, but here and there one could glimpse a broad roof, or a tendril of smoke rising.

"We began with the best of motives," Moros said. "But now I wonder if we got it all wrong."

I could tell Belic had no more idea what he was talking about than I did.

"In our self-interest, we've forgotten what was important."

I was inclined to agree. Making sure your blest horse received food and water on a hot day had to be right up there on the list of most important things, and yet he was clueless. I stamped my hoof and swung my head toward the trough.

The immortal and Belic ignored me. "Look at them," Moros said. By *them*, I knew he meant the poor plebeians who lived in the shadow of Olympus and were subject to the whims of the immortals. Much like we blest horses. "They know nothing of the past. They accept our domination, but not happily. They don't understand why we have the laws that we do. This keeps them more docile. But is it really the right thing to do?"

The right thing to do was tend to your blest horse, I thought.

"I've tried arguing with the others, to no avail. They insist we continue as we have for a thousand years. But my conscience berates me." Moros squeezed his eyes shut. For an immortal being, he looked exhausted. He raised his face to the heavens. "Send me a sign."

Since Zeus was the king of the immortals, I assumed Moros was speaking to him. When no answer came, the immortal turned away. "I need to piss." He walked toward the cover of the trees.

As soon as Moros was out of earshot, Belic leapt into action. He scraped out a message in the gravel that said, *Trust in Henry*. Actually, he wrote *Tryst* first but then realized his mistake and fixed it. I was impressed. I would've guessed he was illiterate.

When Moros returned, the boy "Accidentally" bumped him in order to steer him to where he wrote the message. The immortal stared down at it for a long time before turning to Belic. "You will be our salvation, son," he said.

Heaven help us. I considered scratching an amendment to the message, which would say, *Trust in <anyone but> Henry*. But although the intelligence of blest horses was widely appreciated, no one knew how fully we comprehended human language. And we wanted to keep it that way. Our intellect was both a blessing and a curse. Imagine having a brain full of thoughts just waiting to be communicated, then realizing you have no vocal chords or hands with which to write.

I knew no good would come of trusting Henry-whose-name-was-really-Belic. Yet his antics amused me. I gave silent thanks to the immortals for giving me a sense of humor.

2

RENNIE

Rennie didn't notice how shadowy the room had become until after the dreadful cyclops ate a man. Her heart pounded for the others still captive inside the giant's cave, but she could no longer see the words on the page to find out their fate. To continue, she needed a candle, but she would have to find it without alerting the loremaster. If he saw her, he would force her to go home and spend a sleepless night waiting till she could return and finish Odysseus's story.

She believed the loremaster didn't know she was still here. When she began reading in the afternoon, she had settled on a pillow behind the bookcase and become so engrossed she lost all track of time.

After noiselessly laying down the open volume, she peeked around the corner. Across the corridor, two oil lamps flickered on the table. Neither the loremaster nor his assistant was anywhere in sight. She sprinted to the closest lamp and snatched it up.

"*The Odyssey* will still be here tomorrow," the loremaster said behind her.

THE TRIALS

Rennie spun around. "Please can I finish it tonight?"

His silver earring, shaped like a swan, sparkled in the reflected light. It matched the beautiful embroidery on the collar of his forest green robe. "I'm afraid not," he said.

She knew from long experience when the loremaster was serious. "I'll put it back."

"Leave it to me." He understood her well enough to know she would get caught up reading it again if she went anywhere near the book.

"Good night, Loremaster," she said.

"Sleep well, Rennie."

She would not, of course. How could she sleep without knowing Odysseus's fate? Her shoulders slumped as she crossed the hall and padded out into the sultry summer night. She paused at the bottom of the steps to allow her eyes to adjust to the darkness. Hopefully, the sliver of moon would provide sufficient light to follow the path.

Before she could continue, she heard rapid steps approaching.

"Rennie?" A boy appeared all at once from behind trees.

She stared. He looked like Belic, the older brother of her friend Jennis, yet how could he be? A year ago he'd undergone the Trials. He should be far away from here, serving as a defender to the immortals. Moreover, he appeared to be injured. His arms were wrapped tight around his waist, but she could see where blood had seeped out onto his shirt.

"Is the loremaster inside?" He gave a furtive glance behind him.

"Are you all right?"

"I need to see him right away." His voice faltered. He didn't sound all right.

"It looks like you need a doctor." She noticed something

through the gap in his torn shirt. A sort of medallion made of gold, hanging from a chain.

They both looked back at the sound of trampling hooves. "Over here!" someone called.

Belic's face filled with panic. "I'm too late."

"Come quickly!" Rennie said, regretting her earlier hesitation. "The loremaster is here."

"There's no time. Swear you won't tell them you saw me!"

"But—"

"Swear!"

"I swear!"

Belic fled into the forest, disappearing in darkness. The lights of the horsemen flickered nearer. Any minute, they would reach the gate. She had a moment of indecision, wondering if she should follow Belic's example. But loyalty to the loremaster drove her back into the library so that she could warn him of the danger approaching. When she cried out for him, he appeared almost instantly from his back room. In a frenzied whisper, she explained what had happened during her brief encounter with Belic outside.

The loremaster, small in stature but large in courage, grasped her hand and brought her to a table where *The Odyssey* lay open. "Sit." He took the chair beside her. "If they come in, say nothing of Belic. We've been here alone, reading this book all evening. We haven't seen anyone."

In response to the look of protest in her eyes, he added, "Don't pretend your spine isn't made of steel."

The clomp of heavy boots crossing the threshold made her steel spine turn to jelly, though. A sudden flash of lightning came through the windows and lit up the room, highlighting the grim faces of the three defenders approaching them. A deafening blast of thunder accompanied the entrance of an immortal just behind them. Rennie went cold at the sight of him. She had seen immortals before, but only at the ceremonies, and never from such a close distance. There was no question as to his divinity. His skin was blue where it formed a wide ring around his neck and wrists, and he stood a head above the tallest of the defenders. His black hair matched the tint of his linen shirt and leather pants. Rage seethed from his half-lidded eyes.

"Rise and bow your heads in the presence of the Immortal Ares!" the most ferocious of the defenders shouted.

Rennie nearly fell in her haste to carry out the command. By contrast, the loremaster stood and bowed in a single fluid motion. "My lord, how may we serve you?" he said.

"Search the place," Ares commanded his defenders. They dispersed in three different directions.

"The consequences will be severe if you've hidden the boy," the immortal told the loremaster.

"We haven't seen anyone. I've been reading to this child."

"Girl, did you see the boy?"

Rennie trembled from head to toe as his malignant gaze bore into her. *Never lie to an immortal.* This rule had been drilled into her throughout her life, both at home and at lessons. *An immortal always knows when you are lying.*

Ares exploded at her. "Well, child? Do you dare go silent when questioned by an immortal?"

She was at the brink of admitting everything that had happened outside the library. But at the last second, something gave her the strength to hold back. The fear that Belic would be found and imprisoned or worse. Or maybe it was her instinct that any admission would land her and the loremaster in far worse trouble. After all, he had already told them a lie. "No, my lord. I saw no one," she mouthed through parched lips.

The defenders returned to announce they had searched everywhere and not found him.

Under the heat of Ares's furious glare, Rennie nearly crumpled. He must know that she was lying. Any second, a defender would run her through with a sword before also slaughtering the loremaster for good measure. But somehow, miraculously, Ares charged from the building with his defenders behind him. She still didn't dare move or breathe until another moment passed.

The loremaster spoke first. "I'll take you home. We can leave from the back. There's a chance they might return tonight."

"What will happen to Belic?" she asked.

"His fate is out of our hands."

3

RENNIE

Rennie fixed her gaze on the colossal bronze statue of a blest horse rearing above the altar, thinking of all the times she had wished it would crash down on Moros's head. At first she had feared the consequences of her blasphemy, but no longer. For all the immortals' talk of being omniscient... of hearing every conversation, and divining every thought running through the minds of mortals... Rennie had yet to be struck dead for her transgressions. Her father would say the immortals in their mercy had spared her life. But she had witnessed few, if any, instances of their mercy, and far more of their petty vindictiveness. She could not love them, no matter how hard she tried.

Particularly not Ares after last night. Though Moros wasn't much better, despite having a milder temperament. He appeared to be the oldest, but perhaps not wisest of the immortals. Whereas the others looked as if they would be age forty or so if they were mortal, Moros resembled Mr. Welderby, the cobbler, who had just celebrated his sixtieth birthday. The same gray hair, creased leathery skin, and sour disposition.

Two years earlier, she had watched as he arrived at the stable outside the temple riding his blest horse. On climbing down from the towering animal, the immortal had tumbled on his backside. It was his own fault; the horse had gently crouched to allow him an easy dismount. But after pulling himself up, Moros snatched a whip and slashed at the poor animal several times, drawing blood. The physical wounds weren't deep, but Rennie's heart broke to see the expression of hurt and disappointment that filled the creature's eyes.

She looked back to check if the immortal had arrived. Still there was no sign of him, though the ceremony should've begun a good deal earlier, at the ringing of the mid-morning bell. The residents of Skalbourne had packed themselves thigh-to-thigh on the stiff wooden benches, making the waiting unpleasant to say the least. No one dared talk, but there was much fidgeting, hemming and hawing, and outright wailing from the infants born in the last three months, who had been brought here for the Welcoming.

Rennie despised these affairs. A single baby held no interest for her, never mind dozens of them. One clutched by her mother at the end of the row sounded like a braying donkey. Rennie covered her ear on that side, pretending to itch it, longing for the day when she no longer had to attend. But that wouldn't be for two years, until she turned seventeen and had the excuse of essential work to perform.

When she was young and her mother still alive, Rennie had loved coming to the temple. Its enormous dimensions, carved wooden interior, and flickering candles gave it an aura both comforting and mysterious. She had spent many hours contemplating the glorious stained glass windows that depicted the immortals engaged in noble pursuits. But now she revolted against the temple's grandeur. She believed the intent of its design was to render its mortal occupants insignificant by comparison to their masters.

The need to talk to her sister amplified her usual impatience. Ayva had left the house this morning before Rennie woke up. She usually was an early riser too, but after the encounter with Ares, sleep eluded her for hours, until at last she fell into a fitful slumber just before dawn.

Though Ayva now sat in the pew in front of Rennie, it was not a good time for the sisters to talk. She was leaning against Jarem, with her long silky raven hair captured in a sleek braid and wrapped around his neck. Just when Rennie thought Ayva might turn back and cast her a reassuring glance, she instead pressed her lips to Jarem's ear. Rennie looked away rather than watch her whisper into it, or worse yet, nibble at it.

She missed the time when she and her sister would sit together, pointing out comical situations that would make them both laugh. But for months now, she had barely caught a minute by her side without Jarem suddenly appearing. Rennie had nothing against him per se; he was perfectly nice to her. It was only that she missed having Ayva exclusively to herself.

She could surely arrange for them to have a few minutes alone, if only the ceremony could be done. Rennie swung her head around to glare once more at the entrance to the temple. *Where in Skalbourne was he?*

A moment later, two defenders pulled open the double doors. Surprisingly, it wasn't Moros who strode into the temple, but handsome Apollo. Rennie recognized him though she hadn't seen him since she was a young child.

He bode his time on his way to the altar, smiling left and right, soaking up the adoration of the mortals. Despite her skeptical nature, she couldn't help but find him dazzling. The golden hair fastened in a short ponytail, the fine black leather trousers paired with a shirt made of silk the same color as the rings that marked the skin round his wrists and neck. The identical blue that also matched Apollo's eyes.

At the end of the aisle, he climbed the few steps to the platform from which he looked down on the gathered masses. "Greetings," he said in a rich baritone that resonated across the temple and silenced the squirmers. Even the babies grew quieter, as if they too were eager to hear the immortal speak.

"Welcome! We have gathered here to celebrate Skalbourne's newest arrivals." His eyes focused on a near baby who had broken out into fresh cries, stimulating others to do the same. "Ah, this little fellow is impatient to begin. And who can blame him?"

Polite laughter rippled through the temple. Rennie wondered why Moros hadn't come. He had presided over these Welcomings for as long as she could remember. If he were mortal, looking as old as he did, she would have assumed illness or even death had kept him away today. She wished Apollo had offered an explanation, but his neglecting to do so didn't surprise her. The immortals required no excuses for their actions. If Moros had been feeling a little under the weather, it would be the last thing any of the immortals would ever admit.

Still, she had to wonder if his absence might have anything to do with Belic's furtive return to Skalbourne last night.

"Blessings to the mothers and fathers who brought these precious new lives into Hellas," Apollo continued. "The children gathered here before us are the chosen ones. Formed without defect. The strongest, the healthiest, and the most beautiful. They are the children whose perfection ensures that with each new generation, the Hellenes grow closer to the immortals."

He rambled for several minutes longer, but by now Rennie was tuning out his speech, the same one she had heard countless times before from the lips of Moros. Apollo finished with the immortals' favorite saying: "The immaculate shall inherit the world."

He signaled the parents to bring forth their children and set them on the tables spanning both sides of the aisle. The swaddled infants, realizing rigid wood had replaced their parents' warm embraces, started a new round of screeching. When all were in position, Apollo glided down from the altar and accepted the chalice of holy water handed to him by Minister Reddert. Moving from one screaming infant to the next, the immortal dipped his finger into the water and touched each forehead. He murmured a blessing that Rennie had never been able to hear well enough to understand.

Thank the immortals we're done here. She watched Jarem clasp his hand gently over Ayva's long, slender neck. The two were oblivious to anything outside of themselves.

A sound arose that at first seemed to mingle with the cries of the infants. Seconds later, Rennie realized it came from outside the temple. The sharp, keening wail of a grown person, not a child. Heads whirled in confusion. *Could it be Belic?* No, it sounded like a woman. She knew she should mind her own business, yet somehow, against her better instinct, she found herself rising, squeezing past the others in her row, and hurrying out of the building. Too late, she recalled the immortal must always leave ahead of everyone else. With luck, her lapse had gone unnoticed.

The noise came from a woman bent over at the edge of the forest, near the stable across the road. Moaning now, with her arms clutched around her stomach. As Rennie approached, she recognized Ginna, who had minded Ayva and Rennie for several years after their mother died. Rennie had hardly seen her since then, but the sight of her grief reawakened the feelings of strong affection she had always held for her. She rushed to her side and helped raise her up.

Tears streamed down Ginna's cheeks. "Shhhh, shhhh," Rennie soothed, wrapping her arms around her and rubbing her back. "Shhh, Ginna. The immortals will take offense."

Ginna hiccuped as she struggled to calm herself. "My baby should've been here. They stole him from me. They ripped him from my arms and others held me back till he was gone."

Rennie didn't know she had been with child. "Who tore your baby from you?"

"Defenders, of course. On orders from the immortals."

4

RENNIE

The temple doors came open and Apollo strode out chest first, before pausing to address a group of defenders who stood at attention. Rennie prayed he wasn't instructing them to find the disrespectful girl who slipped out ahead of him.

She drew her former nanny further back behind the trees.

"I wish you could've seen my boy. Lukan. We named him Lukan." Ginna dissolved into a fresh round of weeping. "He looked up in my eyes and I swear, newborn that he was, he smiled at me." A fierce resolve hardened her gaze. "I would've killed to save him. I would've defied the immortals, come what may. I would've. But the defenders were too strong, too fast."

"Shhh, Apollo is near," Rennie whispered. "You couldn't have done anything to stop them." *The immortals choose.* There must've been something wrong with the child. They only take the defectives. Rennie didn't have to ask Ginna what was different about her baby. It didn't matter. What mattered was that she would never see him again.

But Ginna needed to tell her. "So what if his skin is paler than ours, and hair nearly white? His gentle eyes have a pink cast, they said. Why should anyone care? His tiny body is perfectly formed. He can see and hear, and he has a healthy cry. My baby. My sweet Lukan."

Rennie had heard of this before. She wasn't sure what it was called, or what was wrong about it. She only knew the immortals frowned on any condition outside of what was considered normal. *The immaculate shall inherit the world.* She didn't know about that, but clearly it wouldn't be possible for the different to inherit.

She reached for the woman's hand. "Let me take you home."

Ginna shook her head. "Why? So I can stare at the empty crib? Or watch my husband rock in his corner chair in a stupor, saying nothing, doing nothing?"

"Then come to my house."

"No thank you, child." Ginna tightened the shawl around her and escaped through the tangle of trees. Rennie considered calling after her, but what more could she say? How could she console someone who had the worst possible thing happen to them? Only time could heal her grief. If that.

When Rennie turned back toward the temple, she started at the sight of Apollo's blest horse, sniffing the wildflowers outside the stable only a short distance away. She had never been this close to one before. Its size was astonishing, the way it towered above her. Thankfully, it didn't appear to have any interest in her.

Rennie could not take her eyes off the creature. She felt an irresistible desire to approach and caress its golden fur. How incredible it would be to befriend the horse, if that were possible. But only immortals were allowed to touch them. Only immortals could keep them, and place saddles on their backs to ride them. Blest horses were far more intelligent than normal horses, and fiercely protective of their immortal masters. *But it's the mortals who could use some protection*, she thought.

A nervous thrill raced through her as the horse raised its snout in Rennie's direction. She wasn't as frightened as she knew she ought to be, considering how easily the animal could skewer her with a toss of its head, using its short, powerful horn. But she didn't think blest horses attacked without provocation.

The creature shifted attention at the sound of its master approaching. Apollo's eyes were on his horse, and not on Rennie, crouched behind the trees. She held her breath, aware he might spot her in an instant, and who knew how angry he might become? It would seem as if she hid there intending to spy on them.

"Helena, sweet girl." Apollo's manner was gentle. Rennie didn't think he would ever strike his blest horse, as the cruel Moros did. Helena's long tongue unfurled and licked his hand up to the forearm.

"Time to be on our way," he told Helena. Appearing to understand, she crouched to make it easier for him to mount her. He placed a foot in the stirrup, swung onto the saddle, and caught up the reins. But then he hesitated, his attention drawn by a group of stragglers across the road.

Rennie spied Ayva and Jarem among several of their friends. It wasn't possible to miss them, as they both stood out in their own ways. Jarem had a powerful build and an arresting, if not quite handsome face, with piercing black eyes, a hawk nose, and strong cheekbones. Beside him, Ayva was a willowy presence with her tall, slender form and smooth brown skin. Even from this distance, the warmth of her expression and the sweep of her delicate hands marked her as special. But maybe it was only her love for her sister that caused Rennie to view her as a rare orchid among weeds.

Except, it appeared Apollo's gaze was also fixed on Ayva, who was greeting Jarem's mother. It was hard for Rennie to be certain, though, since she had only a sideways view of the immortal. However, when the friends moved away, with a few dropping behind, blocking any further view of Ayva, Apollo lost interest and shifted his attention to his horse. "Let's go." He patted her neck.

The blest horse pounced forward and whinnied sharply at the people remaining in the road, causing them to vault sideways, with several landing in the brambles.

Rennie stepped out from the woods. Apollo's apparent interest in Ayva had left her with a deepening sense of unease.

5

RENNIE

Following a short errand, Rennie quickened her step toward home. On approaching, she assumed Ayva had returned ahead of her and left the door open, but as she drew closer and could see inside, she held her breath. Their possessions were strewn about the place as if a windstorm had passed through the inside of the house.

Seeing large muddy footprints beginning at the entry and heading toward each room, she grabbed a cast iron pan, preparing to defend herself and her sister, if she was here. Drawers were upended on the counter; contents of cupboards taken out and tossed on the floor. Carpets were lifted up and picture frames removed from the walls.

She found their bedrooms in the same disastrous state as the rest of the house. It must've been a parcel of thieves, but unless one of them was still lurking in a closet or under a bed, they had gone away.

"Rennie!" Ayva's voice came from the entry.

The sisters ran into each other's arms. "Are you all right?" Ayva held her tight.

"We've been robbed."

"What did they get?"

"I'm not sure. I'll check the back. You check Poppa's room." Rennie went to the mudroom in the back of the house, where they kept the money used for daily household management in an old metal cup. Someone had emptied it, scattering the coins across the floor. Rennie did a quick count.

"If anything was taken from here, it wasn't much," she called out to Ayva. "I think this is about what we had."

Ayva answered from Poppa's bedroom, where they kept a larger stash in a box under a loose floorboard. "Same here. They found the box, but it doesn't look like they took anything."

"What about your jewelry?" Rennie had none of her own, but her sister had a few pieces of value that came from their mother. She followed Ayva into her bedroom and together they gathered what had been dumped from the jewelry box onto the bed. "It's all here," Ayva said after a moment of searching. "What else do we have that's worth anything?"

"But if they were thieves, why ignore money and jewels?"

It came to Rennie then. They were looking for Belic. Ares must've sent his defenders to search their house for him. Maybe the immortal himself had even entered.

It seemed that Ares knew she'd lied about seeing Belic after all. On top of that, he knew who she was and where she lived too. It was foolish of her to underestimate an immortal. She wanted to kick herself for her stupidity.

But one thing made no sense. Why search the jewelry box, or the small space under a loose floorboard? Her memory flashed back to the glimpse of a gold medallion beneath Belic's shirt. Was that the thing they wanted? Was that the reason Ares himself emerged from Olympus to find the boy?

"We have to clean this up before Poppa gets home." Rennie began hanging Ayva's dresses.

"We need to tell him what happened," Ayva said. "If there are burglars going about ransacking homes, we should warn people."

"We can't tell Poppa."

"We have to! He can protect us." He had influence as head of the council.

"No. Listen to me," Rennie said. "Last night I saw Belic—you remember him? He did the Trials last year."

"Belic? I remember... I didn't know him well. But how could he—?"

"He deserted from the defenders. He came to the library looking for help from the loremaster. But then we heard Ares and his men, and Belic ran off again. It was horrible." Rennie felt sick at the memory. "When Ares arrived, he demanded to know if the loremaster or I had seen him."

"You told him?"

"No. We lied and said we hadn't seen anyone."

Ayva caught her breath. "You lied to the immortal?"

"Yes! See why I can't tell Poppa? He'll throw me out of the house. Worse, he might turn me in to Ares."

The fear was palpable in Ayva's voice. "The immortals know when you lie, Rennie."

"So they say. Maybe that's why they came here and searched. They thought I might be hiding him."

"But what if Ares and his defenders return? Poppa can't help you if he knows nothing about what happened."

"How well do you know our father?"

"Stop it, Rennie."

"He always puts the immortals first. You know it. He'd make me confess."

Ayva chewed on her lip.

Rennie pressed on. "My next stop would be the hangman's post."

"Enough. I won't tell him, as long as we can clean up this mess before he gets home."

They set to work. But after they finished with the drawing room, Ayva sought Rennie to ask her about the matter that continued to puzzle her. "Why do you think Belic deserted?"

"I don't know. His explanation didn't really make sense. But of course, there was no time for him to get into it." Rennie had her own suspicions, though. Before Belic had gone to the Trials, he had been accused of thievery on more than one occasion. The gold medallion he was wearing was not something a defender would be allowed to keep. She suspected he stole it without realizing how significant it was to the immortals. But she held back from discussing this with Ayva. The less her sister knew, the safer she would be.

"I just wonder what could've been so terrible that it drove Belic to desert." Ayva's eyes filled with tears.

"Oh Ayva. Stop. I'm sure nothing like this would ever happen to Jarem."

"I can't help fearing for him. It was bad enough just thinking he might be away for ten years. But what if he suffers?"

"I've been wanting to talk to you about it," Rennie said. "But you seemed all right. I didn't want to upset you by bringing my feelings into it. And now... now the Rite is almost upon us."

"Talk to me about what?"

They drew closer. "I don't know about Jarem. But you...

you're so beautiful. How could the immortals not pick you for a blest? I've tried to put it out of my head, as if that would keep it from happening. But... it will happen. I know it. And then, how am I going to live without you?" Rennie, who rarely cried, erupted in tears. At the Rite, when twelve were picked to undergo the Trials, another smaller group was selected to become blest, and sent to Olympus to serve the immortals, not for ten years, but for the rest of their lives.

"I don't believe they'll pick me," Ayva protested. "The immortals can't have the same opinion of me as you do."

"I saw the way Apollo looked at you today."

"What do you mean?"

"Like you were a piece of meat he was picking out for his dinner."

"Rennie, you can't say things like that!"

"You mean the truth? I've heard rumors about how the blest are required to serve every need the immortals might have. *Every* need."

"It's not true."

"How would you know?"

"How would you?" Ayva glanced at the door, probably to make sure Poppa hadn't returned without anyone hearing. "Of course Jarem and I don't want either of us to be picked."

"You need to run away. It's the only solution."

"Seriously? You know the penalty."

"They can't kill you if they can't find you." If it were her, Rennie thought she would choose death over slavery.

"Do you remember three years ago when Westin ran away? They tracked him down, then a blest horse impaled him..."

"Are you prepared to accept your fate then?"

"There are fifty-seven girls and sixty-one boys. The selections are random. We have as much chance as anyone not to be chosen," Ayva said.

"They say that. I don't believe it. Why is it the most lovely and graceful girls and the fastest, strongest boys are picked? If you won't run away, at least let me try to make you look less pretty."

Ayva rose without answering and returned to the cleaning. Rennie went to work on Poppa's room. She had had her say and could do nothing more. Her sister would do things her own way; she always did.

By the time Poppa came home, they had been finished for half an hour and the sweet loaf Ayva put in the oven was filling the house with a wonderful aroma.

"How was your day, Poppa?" Rennie said.

"Tolerable." His face was more drawn than usual, and for the first time, she thought he looked older than his fifty-two years. When he removed the brimmed hat he insisted on wearing even on the hottest days, it seemed the white hairs were on the verge of overwhelming his original auburn.

"I'll get your tea," Ayva said, ever the attentive daughter.

Rennie joined him at the table. "Has the council decided on the matter of the meeting hall improvements?"

Poppa grumbled. "If you asked them whether the sun would rise tomorrow, they wouldn't agree on the answer. Regarding the improvements, some are against it."

"I imagine the money could be better spent providing food and shelter for those in need," Ayva said.

"My dear, you are always thinking of others. But the truth is, we all benefit when we please the immortals. And they want the improvements."

"What they want, they get. Why even have a council if in the end we must always do their bidding?" Rennie said.

"Watch what you say." Poppa's tone was harsh. "You need to be more respectful or you'll land all of us in a heap of trouble."

"Yes, Poppa." Rennie remembered there was something she wanted to ask him. "Today at the Welcoming, Apollo officiated in place of Moros."

"It isn't for us to question which immortal is in charge of the ceremony."

"I was only wondering if Apollo would be overseeing all our ceremonies from now on."

"I don't know. What difference does it make?"

"He seems very nice. I wondered if he might do the Rite as well." Rennie threw a glance at Ayva to make sure she was listening. If Apollo did the Rite, it was more certain Ayva would be picked.

"The immortals aren't *nice*. They're benevolent."

"I was just thinking he treats his blest horse very well."

"How would you know how he treats his blest horse?"

"I saw him with her after the Welcoming."

"You should mind your own business, Rennie. The immortals dislike being watched too closely by us. It implies a lack of faith on our part."

"I really don't see why they should care one way or the other."

He slammed his fist on the table. "It's not for us to question their desires. They can do whatever they like, say whatever they want, and punish whomever they wish, because they're immortals!"

Rennie knew enough not to continue the conversation any longer. Ayva set his tea down in front of him, calming him. "You're looking healthy today, Ayva," he said.

"Thank you, Poppa."

"In a week's time, we should have a lot to celebrate."

"What do you mean?"

"I think it's fair to say you are the sweetest and most demure of all the girls your age and are likely to be chosen to join the blest."

"Don't say that, Poppa!" Tears sprang to her eyes.

He took her hand. "Calm down, my dear. I know it's hard to think of leaving your sister and me. But there's no greater honor than being chosen. You will in time learn to accept your good fortune."

Rennie watched with a heavy heart as Ayva turned away to hide her weeping and muttered an excuse to leave the room. She cut pieces of Ayva's sweet bread for herself and Poppa, wondering how she would ruin her sister's appearance without him intervening. She didn't know how she could bear it if Ayva was chosen and forced to leave Skalbourne forever.

6

JAREM

Jarem and his mother crossed the meadow dressed in dappled green cotton shirts and brown pants to blend into their surroundings. It was one of the clearest days he could remember, with the dark outline of the forest forming a stark silhouette against the brilliant sky. As beautiful as the weather was, the sun's brutal heat made him wish for clouds. He wiped his sweaty hands against his trousers to dry them, wondering how Mother, wearing gloves and with a kerchief tied around her blond hair, looked as cool as if this were a temperate day in autumn.

He didn't look forward to the hunt. It was rare to see a deer in Gnarl Wood, so their quarry was primarily squirrels, rabbits, and doves. Getting a clean kill of small game could be challenging, and he hated to see the animal suffering, still alive with an arrow sticking out of it. He took his time before shooting to avoid that. Some of his friends viewed hunting as a pleasure, but not him. Hunting and trapping were how his family earned their keep.

They paused near the edge of the wood. Too deep into

the forest, and they wouldn't be able to get a clear shot through the labyrinth of trees. Too distant, and their arrows would fall short of their mark.

As they watched for ripples flowing through the grass, Jarem broached the subject that had been weighing on his mind. "Have you ever thought about us leaving here?"

Mother gave him a sideways glance. "What do you mean?"

"Leaving Skalbourne."

"Where would we go?"

"I don't know. Up north somewhere?"

"What's this about?"

"If we went where no one knows us, we could say Fenn had a recent accident that took away his sight. He could finally live openly, meet other people."

"Life would still be hard for him."

"Sure, but better than being isolated from everyone." Jarem's twin had been born blind. Their mother, widowed a month before the boys were due, decided on her own to keep Fenn alive by concealing his very existence. She bribed the midwife to say nothing, and broke all the immortal laws by failing to declare a defective child, who would not have been allowed to live.

"Assuming I could arrange the move, how would we get Fenn out of here?" Mother said.

"I don't know. Hide him in a burlap sack or something."

She breathed out heavily. "Just when were you thinking about making this move?"

Jarem avoided her eyes. "Before the Rite."

"Is that what this is really about?"

He scowled. "You're not being fair. Ayva and I want to be together for the rest of our lives. If either one of us is chosen, it's over."

"Every mortal must live with this hard truth. The immortals' will takes precedence over our own."

"I won't be happy without her."

"It's up to each of us to find happiness where life takes us," she said. "And if not happiness, then at least satisfaction and meaning."

"You found your happiness by defying the law and keeping your blind baby." Jarem instantly regretted his words, seeing the wounded expression on his mother's face.

She let the remark go. "If we left before the ceremony, we'd have to hide you and Fenn both. You know very well the punishment for avoiding the Rite is death." Her eyes grew damp. "I'm sorry, but I can't bear to risk losing both of you."

Jarem kicked the ground in front of him. "Maybe Ayva and I will ask her father to help us get away."

"Really? Do you know him, Jarem?" This with sarcasm. "He's the head of the council. He lives to serve the immortals. I believe he would turn anyone in to please them. Maybe even his own daughter." A look of panic flashed in her eyes. "You haven't said anything to her about Fenn, have you?"

"Of course not."

"Have you spoken to your brother about any of this?"

He shook his head. "Didn't want to get his hopes up."

"Good."

Movement flashed in front of them. Two fat bickering squirrels ran out from the wood. Jarem raised his bow, but not quickly enough. The squirrels chased each other up a tree and leapt across to another, deeper in the shadows. Darkness swallowed the green glow that surrounded them like a halo.

"I want to tell you something," Mother said. "Not to be repeated to anyone."

Jarem kept his focus on the trees.

"You know your father was older than me. He was on the council when we met. An intelligent but naïve man who hoped to have a positive influence on our way of life. Not long before I became pregnant, a child with a cleft lip was born to an older couple that had no other offspring. At their request, he brought it up at a council meeting, arguing the baby ought to be spared. The child had no more serious condition that might be any threat to generations of mortals, as the immortals like to describe it. The council was swayed and petitioned the immortals. You can guess what their response was.

"Despite this setback, Gregor continued to push for other reforms. He was starting to have an influence; even a few of the immortals seemed to like and admire him. I wondered if he might sway them. And then, three months after you and your brother began growing inside me, your father disappeared. I searched high and low for him without ever finding a clue regarding his fate."

Jarem couldn't believe he was hearing this for the first time. "You told us he died from a fall."

"I was forced to lie by the new head of the council. Word went around that Gregor was found at the bottom of a cliff. I had to bury an empty coffin."

"Empty?" A numbness spread through Jarem. More than once, he had risked exposing Fenn to the world by bringing him to their father's grave that wasn't his father's grave.

"I had to go along with it. If it had only been me, I might've challenged them. But I was with child."

"What do you think happened to him?"

Her face clouded. "He was murdered, and his body

buried to hide evidence of their crime. I'm sure of it. The immortals react swiftly and without mercy to anyone challenging their laws."

"Why didn't they arrest him?"

"He was too popular. It would turn more people against them. They feared they might have a revolt on their hands."

"Why are you telling me now?" Jarem asked.

She put her hand on his shoulder. "You've come of age this year. You're old enough to hear the truth. And if you're picked for the Rite, it could be years before I might get another chance to tell you. It's important to know the crimes of the immortals, especially if you're in their service."

"Do you expect me to avenge my father's death?"

"I expect you to make your own choices based on knowledge, not ignorance."

One of the green squirrels returned, glowing in the shade at the forest edge. Without thinking, Jarem raised his bow, set his arrow, and let it fly. The squirrel leapt to a branch an instant before the arrow would've pierced it.

Jarem drew a second arrow, but paused when he felt his mother's hand press his arm. Her sharp eyes focused on something in the distance. At first glance, it appeared to be a large black cloud, casting a wide shadow beneath it.

"It's a king eagle." Her grip tightened.

The word evoked terror, though Jarem had never witnessed one before. The massive predator soared across the sky, bringing with it the threat of a gruesome death to any creature unlucky enough to fall in its path. Its piercing cry rang out, freezing Jarem's blood.

"Run!" Mother shouted.

7

JAREM

Jarem had almost reached the cover of trees when he discovered his mother was no longer behind him.

He spotted her limping at least thirty feet back, looking like she'd fallen and twisted an ankle. The king eagle was drawing dangerously close. Jarem sprinted toward her, ignoring her attempt to wave him to safety in the other direction.

Despite his fear, he couldn't help admiring the beauty of this colossal bird. Its feathers were a mixture of red and orange and green, and it flapped its enormous wings with magnificent grace. But any second it could choose to dive and snatch up Mother with its massive claws. He reached her side just as the creature flew over them, casting a wide shadow.

"We can't outrun it!" Mother reached for an arrow.

Jarem did the same and aimed for the king eagle's eye, unsure if their arrows might feel no worse than bee stings on any other part of its body.

"Wait!" his mother cried.

The eagle was turning. Seconds later, it headed back the way it had come.

"Let's get out of here," she said. "In case it changes its mind again."

Jarem gave her support until they came to the end of the field. "I can walk now," she said. "It was just a bad cramp in my calf."

Glancing back at the eagle's form receding in the distance, Jarem said, "I thought they died out."

"Apparently not. May the immortals protect us." Her tone conveyed no expectation of their doing so. "Once when I was a child, I saw the silhouette of a king eagle on a moonlit night. That was when they would hunt. It's shocking to see one again after all this time, and even more puzzling to observe it by daylight."

"I haven't heard of anyone being attacked," Jarem said. "Despite the stories me and my friends used to tell around the campfire late at night."

"They prefer deer. It's rare for them to go after humans."

"Deer are scarce these days."

They picked up their pace through the section of terrain known as Granite Gulch. According to legend, the Titans had battled here by hurling the huge rocks and boulders at one another. Jarem and his friends often came to practice climbing and he knew the area well, but his blood froze when he rounded the corner and came face to face with an enormous saddled blest horse. He fell backward as the horse reared up.

"Get back!" his mother shouted at the creature, drawing and setting an arrow.

"Lower your weapon!" Jarem recognized Apollo's voice. "Down, Helena! Down!"

Calming, Helena retreated a short distance.

"How dare you threaten my horse!" Apollo thundered.

"How dare your horse threaten my son!" Mother shouted back.

Jarem watched in disbelief. His mother was going to get both of them killed.

"We came around the corner," Mother continued, "And your horse reared up. I was sure it was going to attack my son."

"You must've frightened her. Why were you running?"

"I'm sorry. Were we supposed to get permission first?"

Apollo looked incredulous at her disrespectful tone. Jarem was certain no mortal had ever spoken to him in such a manner before.

"Mother, please..." Jarem grasped her arm to draw her away.

But when Apollo spoke again, his words were gentler. "I only meant to ask, was there something that caused you to flee?"

Jarem answered before his mother could cause offense again. "Yes, my lord. We saw a king eagle. Please forgive us for startling your horse."

Apollo didn't look surprised by the mention of the king eagle. "Did you see where it went?"

Jarem pointed. "It circled and flew back that way."

Taking her cue from Jarem's polite demeanor, Mother stifled her irritation. "We haven't seen them in years. Do you have any idea why they've returned?"

Apollo shook his head.

"At least now that you know about it," Mother said, "I'm sure we can rely on your protection."

Jarem could only hope her statement sounded sincere to anyone who didn't know her well.

But Apollo laughed. "Maybe we should hire you to

handle the matter. You seem more than capable of taking on this challenge. Or any other."

It was Mother's turn to look surprised, though it didn't stop her from delivering a parting shot. "You're too kind, Apollo. Do we have your permission to continue our journey homeward? And to run if we find ourselves threatened again?"

A flash of annoyance crossed the immortal's face. *Now she's done it*, Jarem thought.

"By all means," Apollo said, "The faster, the better."

"Hurry, Mother." Jarem pulled her arm, afraid she would move at a snail's pace just to prove the immortal had no control over her. But, if only for the sake of her son, she set off at a steady jog and kept it up all the way home.

Fenn had prepared a meal of spiced sausage and beans, one of Jarem's favorites. But the tension he was feeling regarding the approaching ceremony kept the conversation sparse, and Jarem followed his mother's lead in not mentioning the king eagle or the encounter with Apollo.

Jarem did the washing up while Fenn set up the chess board. They played in the evenings when he didn't have plans to meet up with anyone. Skilled at carving and woodwork, Jarem had created the game to Fenn's specifications. The dark squares were slightly raised above the white ones. The pieces had pegs in the bottom that fit into holes on the board, keeping them steady. The tops of the black pieces were rough like sandpaper, while the white tops were smooth, allowing Fenn to tell them apart by feeling them.

Mother had taught them to play when they were little. But it was Fenn who had a natural affinity for the game. Neither had been able to beat him since he turned eight years old. Often he played against himself, and when his opponent was Jarem or Mother, he would constantly suggest better moves than whatever they came up with on their own.

A few moments after the boys settled at the board, Mother announced she was going out to stretch her legs. She loved walking after dark, and on warm nights, she would go for a swim in the lake. *Good.* A chance to speak privately with Fenn, Jarem thought.

Not surprisingly, his brother had the same idea. "What did she say?" Fenn asked.

Jarem had lied to Mother when he told her he'd said nothing to Fenn about his idea of leaving Skalbourne. "I couldn't talk her into it. You know how she is."

Fenn squeezed the bishop in his fist. "Does she have a clue what it's like for me, hiding in that forsaken back room day after day, year after year?"

"She thinks it's a fate better than being executed if we're caught."

"Is it, though? There are times I wish she had just handed me over to the immortals and gotten it over with."

"Who would've taught me chess then?"

"Who's teaching you chess now? You still don't know a damn thing, brother."

This was true. Despite Fenn always demonstrating the smarter moves, he never seemed to get any better.

"What if you're chosen for the Trials?" Fenn said.

"Then I become a defender, or I die."

"You're not going to fucking die. What you lack in brain power, you more than make up for in brawn."

"Nicest thing you ever said to me."

"I mean it. You won't die. But it'll almost be the same thing. At least ten years of servitude. Or a lifetime, if you end up choosing that path."

"I won't, Brother."

THE TRIALS

"It might not be up to you." Fenn looked up with his cloudy, sightless eyes. "What am I going to do without you taking me out of here now and then? That's the only reason I'm still sane."

They sometimes went out after midnight when no one was about. In the summer, they'd go to the lake for a swim. In the winter, if they were lucky enough that snow came, they would sled down the nearest hill and pummel each other with snowballs. And now and then, when the mood hit them, they went to the cemetery to talk to their father by the side of what they had believed to be his grave. *What Fenn still thought of as his grave.* Jarem needed to confide in his brother about this, but now didn't feel like the time.

"Mother has never taken me anywhere, and never will," Fenn said.

Jarem moved his knight and told Fenn the new position. Fenn picked it up and moved it back. "Trust me, Brother. Look at your rook."

Jarem saw what he meant.

"Who's your best friend?" Fenn said.

"Huh? You, I guess."

"After me."

Jarem thought about it. "Ayva. Yeah, definitely her."

"Tell her about me. Ask if she'll sneak over now and then to take me out."

"I can't do that."

"You'd do as much for a fucking dog."

"It wouldn't be dangerous for a dog."

"Seriously," Fenn continued. "I'm just asking for one friend while you're away. Are you afraid she'll fall in love with me instead?"

"Don't kid yourself." Fenn's appearance didn't bother Jarem, but he was certain the sight of his brother's eyes, which had a strange, milky-white surface, would repulse any other person. The community had little tolerance for defectives, even when their condition was caused later in life by illness or accident.

"Then why not tell her about me?"

"She might be chosen too. Very likely as a blest."

"But what if she isn't? Is it because you don't trust her with the secret of me? You think she'll tell someone?"

"I would trust her with my life."

"Then trust her with mine," Fenn said.

8

I, ASTERIOS

I woke in a foul mood. For several days now, I had been cooped up in the small pasture adjoining the stable. Moros normally took me out for daily walks, but he had not come since Belic wrote that ridiculous message, "Trust in Henry." I could not help but wonder if that had anything to do with the immortal's absence.

Mostly I was upset with Apollo, however. He claimed to love his blest horse, Helena, and yet off he went, forcing her to carry his heavy weight on her back, and she with child. In fact, she was due to deliver any day now.

Helena was my daughter. For reasons unknown, blest horses did not produce live offspring very often, and therefore she was my only child. As long as Apollo did not ruin things with his constant demands on her, this foal would be her first and perhaps also the only one. Three times in the past, she had miscarried.

I knew I ought to at least walk around the pasture and exercise my legs a bit. Instead, after Ethan, the stable master, let me out of my stall, I shuffled to Helena's empty enclosure and smelled her scent. This had a soothing effect, but it wasn't the same as standing beside her and laughing when she teased the stable hands by pretending to misunderstand them in ridiculous ways.

"Okay, that's enough moping," Ethan said a little while later. "It's a beautiful day. Get your ass out there."

Since Ethan had spoken to us like this ever since we were colts and fillies, we let him get away with it. We also allowed him and his stable hands to touch us. If any other mortal tried that, I'd be obliged to use my horn. The last time I poked someone, it felt like just a tap on my end, but the mortal ended up with several broken ribs.

I trotted outside and did a few laps around the pasture past several mares congregated in the eastern corner. I could hear snippets of the thoughts they were sharing about that rogue, Petros, father of my daughter Helena's child due to be born any day now, and supposed mate to the young mare, Ismene. We blest horses had the ability to project our thoughts and sensations to others of our kind. This didn't mean that any passing filly had access to my innermost secrets, fortunately. We could project or not project as the mood suited us. Proximity was a factor as well; these days I practically needed to be within spitting distance to hear anything. The horse I most wanted to communicate with—Helena—was way too far away in Skalbourne.

Annoyed by the mares' idle gossip, I moved on. Eventually I paused to stare at the road leading down toward the valley, wondering if my grandchild might already have been born. Ethan approached carrying half a watermelon.

"I know you're worried about that sweet girl of yours. But Apollo assured me he wouldn't ride her hard and promised extra pampering after the birth." He explained everything to me like he knew I could understand every word, although he had no such awareness. He used to talk the same way to his dog, and once I even heard him telling a chicken the reasons why it would be better off not crossing the road. In time, I decided he was just one of those mortals who valued all living creatures the same and felt they deserved explanations whether they understood them or not.

Still, his assurances regarding Apollo fell on deaf ears. The immortal's actions were unforgivable.

Ethan took out his long knife from its sheath, cut the watermelon in large pieces, and lay them down before me. "Eat up, old man."

Although the aroma of sweet watermelon nearly overwhelmed my reserve, I continued to hold back.

"Nothing better than tasty food to soothe an ailing heart," he said.

I raised my head, aloof, as Ethan returned to the stable.

All at once, I heard stampeding hooves coming toward me from the side. Before I could react, Petros sideswiped me, nearly knocking me over. I neighed furiously, raised up on my rear legs, and battered him with my front hooves. He backed away, knowing better than to get into it with me. I might be old, but I was taller and stronger than the young blest horse. Admittedly, I had far less endurance, but for a quick bout, I was the likely victor.

It was clear he'd been trying to snatch away my watermelon. Projecting my thoughts, I said, *I might share if you tell me where you went with Ares today.* I hoped he would have news of Helena.

Petros neighed and bucked his rear legs. He was full of youthful pride and aggressiveness, just like his master. But a moment later, his head cooled, and he responded to me. *Moros says crazy shit. Other immortals don't like it.*

Petros's language skills were not the best. His name

meant *stone* and I thought that described the state of his mind fairly well.

He says the same crazy shit to the kid too, Petros continued.

I knew he meant Belic.

Other immortals barred Moros from leaving his stall, he said. I interpreted this to mean they had locked Moros into his apartments.

They were going to send the kid to the mines, but he escaped. We chased him to Skalbourne.

Did you find him? I asked.

Not yet. Zeus is enraged. He sent a king eagle.

A king eagle? I wondered if I had interpreted his words correctly.

Right. A king eagle. You know. A big bird? Really big.

I never saw one before but had heard the immortals speak of them. They followed commands from Zeus, but no other. For the first time, I felt sorry for Belic. A king eagle would tear the boy to shreds as if he were no more than a helpless fly.

Did you see Apollo and Helena? I asked.

Petros shook his head.

I pushed the watermelon toward him and let him eat all of it. His words had not been reassuring. Would I ever see Moros again? And if not, what would happen to me? All the other immortals had their own blest horses. Heaven forbid I should be designated as a *spare.* I knew Moros's habits and preferences intimately. I did not love him, but there was a lot to be said for consistent behavior. Other immortals could be unpredictable and therefore dangerous. I did not wish to spend my golden years jumping at shadows.

But what could I do? I was only a blest horse, subject to the whims of the immortals.

9

RENNIE

Rennie rose early, lit her candle, and made the mistake of glancing in her mirror. It was annoying how her untamed red hair sprang out in all directions like a lion's mane after a night's sleep. She yanked it all back from her face and tied it into a ponytail. Once she had tried cutting it below shoulder-length, but that only meant it was too short to secure it and therefore she had to wear a hat for three months. She hadn't cut it since then and now her hair fell to midway down her back.

She put on her light pants with big pockets—unlike Ayva, Rennie never wore skirts—and a sleeveless blouse in anticipation of another hot day. In the kitchen, she prepared tea, a boiled egg, and toast for herself, being careful not to wake Poppa. Though Ayva was normally up at the same time, she didn't come out from her room. Likely she was sleeping in after a restless night filled with foreboding over the approaching ceremony.

With practiced stealth, Rennie slipped outside and closed the door silently behind her. It gave her a sudden chill to imagine that Ares or his men might be watching her in case she might lead them to Belic. She checked around the house for them, but finding no signs of anyone, she set off along the forest path that would get her to the library fastest. The rising sun made her squint as it shone through the gaps in the trees. She had chosen this time because the loremaster always unlocked the front entrance shortly after dawn. He typically left at midday for a meal and a rest before returning for the remainder of the afternoon and evening.

An unusual stillness hung in the air this morning. Missing were the sounds of the wind riffling the leaves or swishing the branches. The birds did none of their usual chirping and bickering. The crows normally threw a fit of cawing if anyone passed near their nests, but not today. Even the glow squirrels remained in hiding.

It was probably the heat. Though the sun had barely risen, the temperature was already uncomfortable enough to cause sweat to bead on her forehead. No wonder the animals were subdued today.

She wiped her face with her handkerchief before knocking at the library door. No one answered at first, which was unusual. She knocked harder twice more before the loremaster's assistant opened the door just a crack.

"The library is closed." Kern, a round-faced lad of twelve, still spoke in a high-pitched voice despite his efforts to mimic the loremaster's diction.

"It is? Why?"

"We are closed for repairs."

"Repairs? I need to talk to the loremaster. Please let me in."

"My apologies, but—"

"Let her in." The loremaster's voice came from inside the building.

Kern made a face at being overruled before pulling the door fully open for Rennie.

She now understood why Kern had said the building was closed. The library, at least one side of it, looked very much as her house had yesterday. Someone, or a group of someones, had toppled the shelves and knocked down all the books. It tore Rennie's heart to see the ripped pages and broken bindings that resulted.

The loremaster approached. "This occurred while I was walking you home two nights ago. We've been working hard to restore order since then." This explained the section of the library that looked normal.

"Somebody came to my house during the Welcoming and did the same," Rennie said.

His expression darkened. "I had no idea. I didn't think they knew who you were."

"You didn't tell them?" *Of course he didn't.* She regretted the question as soon as she saw the hurt flash in his eyes.

"Come with me." He led her to his private room in the back and shut the door behind them. "Sit down."

After they both were seated, the loremaster spoke to her in a lowered voice. "Do you have any idea what they were looking for?"

"The boy. Belic."

"I don't believe they would search for a person between the pages of a book."

"Maybe we angered the immortal and this was his retribution," Rennie whispered.

The loremaster kept his gaze on her, waiting for more information. But Rennie did not tell him about the medallion.

"You came here to speak with me?" he said after a moment.

"Yes. Not about this. I have a question." She fiddled with her handkerchief, avoiding his eyes. "Do you have any maps of Hellas?"

A silent pause followed before he slowly rose and retrieved a rolled parchment from a large drawer behind his desk. "You may have this." He spread it out on his desk.

The map showed Skalbourne, where they lived, along with the major towns of Barmwich and Hardwaite to the north. In between lay several minor villages where presumably a traveler could find food and lodging en route. To the south, the vast emptiness known as the Savagelands was indicated on the map. Olympus fell to the east, in the foothills of the great mountains.

Rennie frowned. "This doesn't show any of the walking trails or the, um, alternate ways in and out of the larger towns." *Unguarded holes in the walls and fences, in other words.*

"No, it does not."

"What about the Savagelands? Are there no roads there?"

The loremaster cleared his throat. "Does your interest in hidden routes have anything to do with the upcoming Rite?"

Rennie stared past him at a black fingerprint on the white surface of the wall, pondering. *Truth or a lie?*

"I know your sister Ayva is of age," the loremaster continued. "I'm sure she would never consider shirking her duty, but if the thought did occur, I would advise against it in the strongest terms. The immortals ruthlessly pursue anyone on the current year's birth rolls who is not present at the ceremony."

"But Loremaster, what if she's forced to join the blest?"

"Would she prefer to die? Because that will be the result if she is caught trying to escape."

Rennie lowered her voice. "Some things might be worse than death."

"Hush, child. You're way too young to be giving up on life."

A shudder ran through her at the memory of Ares' wrath. "Do you know if they're still looking for Belic?"

"I haven't heard that he was found." The loremaster lowered his gaze and exhaled. When he raised his eyes again, he said, "There's a man named Rhomer who often sells leather goods at Skalbourne Market. He can help you with the information you seek... if he chooses."

"What does he look like?"

"He is... unremarkable. Deliberately so, I imagine. Medium height and weight. Light brown hair and light brown skin. Plain clothing. He dresses in a way that doesn't call attention to itself."

"Thank you, Loremaster." Rennie stood up.

"Not having children of my own, I feel as a parent toward many of you. Please tell your sister I urge her to attend the Rite as required."

10

RENNIE

Returning home, Rennie followed the longer path that had a berry patch along the way. The blackberries ought to be ripe now, and if the birds had not eaten them all, she would gather some for Ayva to make into a pie. She didn't have the patience for cooking, but her sister had a rare talent for it. Ayva would do well to seek work as a baker, assuming the worst didn't happen and she would not be compelled to wait on the immortals in Olympus.

Although it was well into morning, the forest continued to feel stifling, as if an invisible shroud had been lowered over it. She tried to shake off the breathless sensation. Her worry about the upcoming ceremony was playing tricks with her mind.

Coming to the blackberries, she laid her handkerchief on the ground underneath the bush to collect them. The birds had already snatched most of the ones from the outer branches, but with some effort, she gathered enough from the back. When she had the amount needed for two pies, she wrapped up the cloth and tied it to her belt.

Before long, she noticed a stench that reminded her of meat left out of cold storage for too long. It worsened with each step she took, until she became convinced someone or something must have died in the vicinity. Her hands grew clammy at the thought of some kind of predator nearby, and a powerful urge to turn back nearly overcame her. But she needed to confirm whether the dead thing was a person, because, of course, in that case, she would have to report it to the captain of the defenders.

She forced herself to continue until a clearing opened and in the middle of it, a thick undulating cloud of black flies topped an enormous mound of *something*. She blinked before realizing with a shock that it was a blest horse. The creature lay sprawled on the forest floor, its torso open with a ragged gash running the length of it. Bits of its entrails remained, but it appeared the bulk of the horse's internal parts were missing. Eaten, probably. But by what? What creature had the power to overcome a blest horse?

That thought alone would've sent her racing back the way she came if she hadn't heard a high-pitched whinny just then. Was there *another* horse, one that was still alive? Her curiosity propelled her forward.

Getting a closer look at the dead horse, she saw it was Helena, the one belonging to Apollo. She recognized her from the unusual white patch of fur she had between her eyes. Everywhere else, her fur was a golden hue, like that of other blest horses.

Another whinny came from the far side of the corpse. She followed the sound to a delicate foal, which could be less than an hour old for all she knew. The baby, standing awkwardly on spindly legs, nudged its mother repeatedly with its nose, where there was a bony nub that would eventually grow into a powerful horn.

Poor thing. Rennie ached to comfort it, but the immortals forbade anyone from touching their precious animals. Her chest tightened when the little foal looked up at her with pleading eyes. "I wish I could bring your mother back to life, but I can't."

The colt—she could see its gender now—clambered to his feet and stumbled cross-legged toward Rennie. He sniffed in the direction of the blackberries.

"Are you hungry?" She took out a few and dropped them on the ground. The colt scooped them up with one swipe of its tongue, before raising eyes hopeful of another serving.

"Maybe this was not a good idea." Nevertheless, she was about to offer more when she heard voices and movement in the distance. "Shit," she hissed to herself. The noise increased as the strangers drew closer.

With only seconds to spare, she spotted a possible hiding place and raced toward it, skipping to avoid leaves that might crunch loudly under her feet. She threw herself under a leafy bush and crouched in the hollow behind it. But when she looked back, she discovered to her horror that the colt had tunneled in after her. "Go away," she whispered. "You can't stay here."

Predictably, the horse didn't follow her directions, and instead nudged Rennie's hand with his head, making her drop the packet of blueberries. They all tumbled out. *I'll never get rid of him now.*

A small gap in the branches allowed Rennie to glimpse movement in the clearing. She trembled to think this group must be searching for Helena and the colt. He was occupied eating the fruit, but she feared that when he finished, he would wander out and draw attention to their hiding place. If she were discovered, it would seem as if she had been trying to kidnap him.

From the clearing came a grief-stricken moan. With a shiver of fear, Rennie recognized Apollo's voice. "Helena. *No.*"

Whoever was with him knew better than to say anything. It sounded as if Apollo might be weeping.

"How... how did she get here?" he asked a moment later in a voice filled with mingled grief and rage.

"Broke out of her stall, my lord."

"Now why would she do that?"

"I don't know, my lord." The tremulous way he spoke made Rennie picture the defender with his head lowered and hands shaking.

"You know there was a king eagle spotted in the area?" Apollo demanded.

"Yes, my lord."

King eagle? They were the stuff of nightmares. Rennie had never seen a live one; only an illustration in a book. Until now, she wasn't certain if they were real or legend.

"Where's the foal?" Apollo said.

Sounds of movement followed. "Not inside her," the man said.

"Then it may be here. Look around."

"For the foal, my lord?"

"Didn't I say that?"

Footsteps crunched over the pine needles.

The hair rose on Rennie's arms. There was nowhere else to hide, and no possibility of running without being seen. If they kept searching, they would eventually come upon them, or the colt would make noises drawing their attention. It would look exactly like she was trying to steal him. She even had a kerchief stained with blackberry juice, obviously meant to lure him away. They would kill her for this. There was no way around it.

The foal, having lost interest in the remaining fruit, let out a soft snort.

"Did you hear something?" Apollo said.

"What sort of sound, my lord?" the man said.

"I'm not sure."

Rennie had a desperate thought. She had heard before that the beating of their mother's heart was a comforting sound to mammals. Carefully, gently, she wrapped her arms around the colt's head and drew him against her breast.

"The king eagle may have taken the foal to its nest," Apollo said. "If we hasten, we might save it."

Rennie couldn't imagine how Apollo's defenders could find the nest, which was probably perched high on the edge of a cliff at the very top of a mountain somewhere. She gazed down at the sweet baby pressed against her. His breathing thickened and his eyelids lowered.

The footsteps drew nearer to her hiding place. The colt opened his eyes and wiggled his nose, sniffing. She held her breath.

A tense moment passed. "He's not here," Apollo said. "Certainly not alive. He wouldn't stray from his mother if he was. Return to Olympus and fetch a conveyance to transport her back home. She'll get a royal burial."

After the sounds of their departure died down, Rennie emerged from her hiding place and headed toward the path that led home. The colt followed her.

11

TOMMIS

Tommis slithered into the crawl space under the building to check his bait. Yesterday he had planted ten pieces of arsenic-laden cheese there. Creeping on his hands and knees across the dirt, he discovered three rat corpses, including a full-sized adult and two juveniles. He shoved them into his sack before scanning further to confirm none of the poison remained. There could be other dead bodies outside, but not around the dressmaker's shop, because he had scoured that area first. His pa taught him long ago that rats upset the customers, particularly the female ones, and therefore he must always move them out of sight as quickly as possible.

Pulling himself up from the bowels of the building, his spirits plunged to see the two people he would least like to encounter right now. *Ayva and Jarem.* She looked like a goddess in a bright yellow dress with a garland of flowers in her hair, and Jarem wore this smug expression like he *thought* he was an immortal. They were holding hands and practically skipping, until they saw Tommis covered in mud from head to toe, carrying a stinking sack of dead rats. They stopped dead, staring at him like he was no better than one big giant rat himself.

Ayva recovered first. "Oh, hi Tommis." Then, maybe because she wanted to be nice but couldn't think of anything else to say, she asked, "What have you got there?"

Tommis stood there speechless and gaping like a demented grandparent. *Poisoned rats. Do you want a peek?*

"Ayva, you know what he does," Jarem said.

"Oh, that's right, well, I hope you caught plenty because I think I'd scream if I saw one in the dress shop."

"We need to get going," Jarem told her.

"I bought this from your mother." Ayva pointed out her flower garland to Tommis. "Do you like it?"

Jarem saved Tommis from having to reply. "For immortals' sake, Ayva, must everyone admire you?"

Her expression sank, and she lowered her voice as they started across the road. "Why do you have to be so mean?"

"Sorry. I'm just, you know... there's a lot going on."

A lot going on. Tommis couldn't imagine what excuse Jarem had to be upset about anything, as long as Ayva continued to dote on him. Jarem, who had nothing to recommend him aside from a swaggering overconfidence, somehow believed he held the right to scold her instead of kissing the feet she walked on.

It still pierced Tommis's heart to remember the day two years earlier when he'd come upon them just off the main path in Gnarl Wood, with Jarem's mouth assaulting hers and his arms squeezing her, with one hand sneaking under her blouse in the back. Tommis had barfed into the pine needles before doubling back the way he'd come.

Once he had been deluded enough to believe he might gain her love someday. When they were both eleven years old, he'd had the good luck to come upon her at the same moment a snake plunged from an overhead branch, landing on her shoulder. The viper was perfectly harmless, but she still screamed as if it were Medusa's decapitated head. Tommis had swooped in from behind, snatched its tail, and flung it into the forest. Ayva had wrapped her arms around him in grateful relief.

From then on, she had dropped by his house every week with home-baked treats like biscuits and sweet breads and her special toffee best of all. At school she had chattered happily to him whenever they shared a moment alone, showing no regard for the opinions of others who mocked him for being the ratcatcher's son.

For weeks before discovering her in Jarem's embrace, Tommis had been struggling to find the courage to kiss her. Afterward, he cursed himself day and night for not acting sooner. The food gifts ceased and while she still addressed him cordially, her voice carried no more warmth than what she expressed to virtually every other person who crossed her path.

Looking down at his dirty, disheveled self, wearing threadbare pants split at the knees, he couldn't blame her. Associating with him would only bring shame upon her. The same shame he felt for himself and his profession on a daily basis.

Thankfully, this was his last job for the day, and if everything went as he hoped, he wouldn't have to put up with any of this much longer. He disposed of the dead animals before heading back, but the familiar sensation of dread filled him the closer he got to the dilapidated two-room shack they called home. *What would Pa's mood be today?*

The answer came swiftly. "Tommis?!" Pa shouted from the back room where he and Ma had their bed. From long experience, Tommis could tell he was already drunk. "Tommis, get in here!"

He felt sick to his stomach, but there was no avoiding Pa's commands as long as he lived in this house. He found his father slumped in bed, an empty pitcher beside him. His eyes were bleary and he stank of liquor. "Let's have it then. Today's earnings." He slurred his words as was often the case.

Tommis emptied his pockets onto the table beside his father. "What, is this all?"

"Yeah it is."

His father moved surprisingly fast for a bulky, inebriated man, leaping up, grabbing Tommis by the collar, and shoving him against the wall. The boy's head banged hard against it.

"You better not be holding out on me. This can't be everything."

"It is. I swear it."

Pa slapped him across the face. Tears sprang to his eyes but Tommis bit his lips to hold them back.

"You still say there's no more?"

"Yeah, Pa." Tommis steeled himself, anticipating another blow, but his father fell back on the bed, already worn out from his exertion.

"You need to catch more rats. Never going to get enough with poison alone. Farnsworth uses ferrets."

They had been over this many times before. "They'll cost us. And last time we tried one, the ferret ran away."

"That's cuz you didn't keep a close watch on it! So many excuses. Fact is, the town needs more vermin for you to catch. Bring a couple live rats home next time. A male and a female, mind you. Start breeding 'em."

This was another of his favorite schemes. He was in top form today.

"Okay, Pa," Tommis said. It paid to go along with whatever he said, because he would certainly forget the agreement by morning.

The outer door creaked open and they heard Ma entering the front room.

"Ginger!" Pa said. "Come here!"

A moment passed before she shuffled across the threshold. With her nervous glances and skittish movements, she appeared even more mouselike than usual. She was always on the lookout to flee at a second's notice. This was what living with Pa had done to her. "I'm home from the market," she said.

"Okay, Mrs. Obvious, let's see your earnings." Pa spread his greedy paw to receive the contents of Ma's purse, mostly pennies earned from selling her flowers today. "Between the two of you, we're going to starve."

"You'll be feeling better soon," she told him. "You can go back to work."

"Just how am I going to do that with this foot?" He stuck it in the air. Three weeks earlier he had bruised it slightly, but from what Tommis could tell, it had healed shortly after.

"Well, you'll need to, won't you? The Rite is almost here. What if Tommis is picked?" Ma said.

"Our son? He won't be picked. Are you crazy?"

"They pick them at random. Unless they have twelve volunteers. I don't think that's ever happened."

"Don't care if he's picked, he's not going."

Tommis shrank back against the wall while they continued to discuss him as if he wasn't there.

"If he's picked, he has to do the Trials. That's the law," Ma said.

Tommis could see Pa struggling for a comeback to this. Finally he said, "He won't be picked," as if by pronouncing his desire, he could make it true.

"He might want to volunteer."

"You're out of your mind. He's not going to volunteer. Anyway, I won't let him."

Tommis caught his breath. *Won't let me?* As far as he knew, no one could prevent him from volunteering. Since the idea was first suggested to him, he had been dead set on carrying it out.

"You sure he needs your permission?" Ma said.

"You questioning me?" Pa gave her his threatening glare. He looked around, recalling Tommis was in the room. "Don't know why we're even discussing this. You go to the Trials, you're not coming back from them alive. I was lucky and didn't get chosen. My youngest brother, not so lucky, and him a puny little kid. Couldn't keep up. They say he was torn limb from limb."

Tommis had heard this gruesome story many times before. In every telling of it, Pa showed no signs of grief whatsoever, just a morbid fascination regarding his brother's fate.

Pa leaned back and closed his eyes. All this talk after all that liquor had been too much for him. Tommis slipped out of the room and then out the front door. He felt like throwing up. This was the first he had heard that his parents' permission might be required. *Is it true?* He needed to find out as soon as possible. And if so... if he didn't become one of the few to be randomly picked... if he didn't get his chance to undergo the Trials... his life was over. He might as well end it after that.

12

TOMMIS

Tommis sprinted all the way to Council Hall. If they closed and he couldn't find out till tomorrow whether permission was required, he would have a sleepless night. He arrived just as a middle-aged woman wearing a fuzzy pink cape was closing up the building. "Come back tomorrow," she said in clipped tones, like someone accustomed to reminding others regarding the rules.

"It's just a quick question. Do I need my parents' permission to volunteer for the Trials?"

"Come back in the morning and submit your question in writing."

"But why can't you--"

The woman laughed. "I was only joking. The child does not require his or her parents' permission in advance; however, if a parent were to object directly after the fact, the child's voluntary request to become one of the selected would be denied. It wasn't always this way, mind you. But after years of children volunteering without their parents even knowing about it, and then dying on the battlefield of their innocence, so to speak... the immortals in their mercy set down the requirement."

The immortals in their mercy... mercy to whom? Tommis spun around to hide the disappointment on his face. He heard the city official mutter something about the ingratitude of young people.

He walked for a long time having no idea where he was going. It didn't matter, as long as it wasn't his own home. He couldn't face his father right now, though he knew he would more than pay for his absence tomorrow.

After hours of wandering, Tommis's feet dragged him to the statue of Zeus outside the temple. He had been coming here since he was a little boy to pray to the immortals and beg them to save him from his father. His praying made no difference in his life, and yet he persisted, until at last, three months ago, he had a divine encounter.

She had arrived on her magnificent blest horse, galloping down the road, then veering toward Tommis at the base of the statue. He had leapt to his feet, ready to bolt, but she called out, telling him to wait, and he knew better than to defy the command of an immortal, even if she appeared ready to run him over with her mount.

But the horse did stop well before reaching Tommis, and the immortal named Aphrodite poured from her saddle like melted butter. Her looks were arresting, from her lofty height to her slender form, proud demeanor, and mane of red hair tumbling in unruly curls over her shoulders. She wore a flowing tunic and trousers in a shade of blue matching the pigment of her skin that formed colored rings round her neck and wrists.

He didn't quite believe she could be real, but a vision sent by the immortals was just as good, in his mind.

She greeted him in a friendly tone and asked his name.

"Tommis, my lady," he said.

Staring at him, she wiggled her earlobe. "What happened here?"

He wanted to respond, but he didn't know what she was talking about.

"Your ear. Did an animal attack you?"

Of course. He had been missing the lobe of his left ear for so long, he sometimes forgot about it. Naturally, she knew he must not have been born like that or his life would've been forfeited.

Strictly speaking, it *was* an animal that attacked him. Fearing she might demand to know *what* animal, he said, "No, it was an accident."

"What sort of an accident?"

"Um... I fell and..." He fumbled over his words, struggling to come up with a story. *Fell and landed on a knife that cut through my ear?* Already her eyebrows were arched in a skeptical look.

"You know you must tell me what really happened. You cannot lie to the immortals."

It was a crime that could be punishable by death to refuse to answer an immortal, or to lie to one. Still, it was hard to get the words out. He'd told no one before. "Someone cut it off," he murmured.

"Who cut it off? Who would do such a thing to a child?"

"My... my... my father." He spoke in such a faint whisper he didn't think she would hear him. But she did.

"Your father?" She shouted the words, causing Tommis to cringe in horror. *What if anyone hears her? What if Pa finds out I told?*

"Why on Olympus did he do that?"

"I made him angry."

"What did you do?"

The truth was, he no longer remembered. He didn't think it was anything all that terrible, certainly not worthy of an ear being cut off. But Pa's furies were unpredictable and often out of all proportion to the offense committed. "I don't remember."

"Never mind then. I'm sorry your father is such a brute."

He lowered his head, feeling ashamed of both himself and Pa.

"Have you come here to pray for his death?"

The question shocked him. He wondered if she was testing him.

"Well?" she said.

"No. I prayed… that he wouldn't hurt me anymore."

"Oh, that's very much the same thing, I suppose. How old are you?"

"Sixteen."

"Then you can volunteer for the Trials. Once you become a defender, he can no longer harm you."

"I guess."

"Yes, that is what you must do." She had mounted her horse without another word and ridden away, as if the matter were settled. She left Tommis trembling in disbelief over her interest in him. He found a stick and jabbed himself hard enough to draw blood to be certain he wasn't dreaming.

Since then, he had seen her ride past two more times while he was praying at the statue, but she didn't stop to speak to him on those occasions. Maybe because she thought he was all set. He would volunteer and that would be that. She didn't appear to know his parents' permission was required.

With no more options remaining, he had returned to Zeus's feet tonight to beg once more for the immortals' intervention. The tears he had held back all day burst forth.

He didn't hear Aphrodite behind him until she spoke. "Tommis, you're too old for all this weeping."

Springing to his feet, he stifled his tears and wiped his face with his shirt before bowing to her. "I beg your pardon, my lady. I didn't hear you approach."

"You should be happy. The Trials are almost upon us. You're not frightened of dying, are you? It's hard, of course, but it's not exactly what Odysseus was forced to endure."

"My father won't let me volunteer. The council official said he has to allow it."

"Well then, if the official said so..." Her tone was mocking.

"Was she wrong?" A pinprick of hope entered Tommis.

"Oh, I imagine she was right. I don't keep track of all the little rules and regulations. But I'm sure she does."

Just as quickly, Tommis's hopes deflated.

"Well, are you just going to give up?" she said.

"I guess there's a slight chance I'll be picked and called to the Trials."

"Don't ever leave anything to chance. Only the weak do that. And it never turns out well for them."

He didn't know what to say to this.

"Is your mother opposed to your wishes too?"

"No. She wants me to be happy."

"All right then. It's only your father standing in the way."

"Only?"

"You have just one obstacle to achieving your dream. Just one. How hard can it be to remove it?"

"What do you mean?"

She raised her eyebrows in a knowing look. "Let go of sentimentality, self-blame, and assumptions based on what you've been taught. Place your trust in the immortals." Beautiful Aphrodite departed on her magnificent horse, leaving Tommis to ponder her words, wondering if she knew what had happened to Winom. *Immortals are all-seeing and all-knowing.* Yet, would she be so quick to resolve him of blame if she had witnessed his actions on the day his brother died?

13

TOMMIS

It must've been well past midnight when Tommis left the temple and set off toward home. Exhaustion had finally caught up with him, and he wanted nothing more than to collapse onto his small pad in the front room and sleep for hours. He would wait to consider his next steps until after he was well-rested.

Halfway there, he noticed a young woman walking ahead of him along the side of the road. A moment later, as she passed under a shaft of moonlight, he recognized her as Ayva. She paused and glanced all around as if nervous of anyone seeing her. He ducked behind a tree just in time to avoid detection, and when he dared to peek out at her again, she was turning onto a path.

Where could she be going alone at this hour of the night? He hastened to where she had left the road and glimpsed the back of her, just before she rounded a corner and disappeared from view.

He padded onto the path after her. A tremendous curiosity drove him forward, along with no small desire to protect her. He knew this route. For now, he could keep well behind her without fear of losing her. In a little while, when they neared the next crossing, he would need to draw closer to see which way she went.

Before he reached it, though, he spotted her paused ahead, standing with a boy who was almost certainly Jarem. His heart sank with disappointment. He had assumed this was something else. If they were going to sneak out late to see each other, why not do it closer to one of their homes?

Tommis was about to turn back when another boy emerged from behind a tree. Ayva cried out and stumbled backward, while Jarem appeared unsurprised. In fact, he must've brought this person with him, because he reached for the boy's arm and pulled him nearer.

That Jarem would invite another boy to his assignation with Ayva piqued Tommis's curiosity further. He could not leave without at least attempting to learn more. From his job catching rats, he was rather good at creeping about. Fortunately, the wind, which had picked up in the last hour, caused sufficient noise to cover the sounds of his slithering across the forest floor. Before long he was near enough to make out their conversation.

By peering through the branches from his new vantage point, he got a close up view of the two boys. He blinked, wiped his eyes with his sleeve, and looked again, wondering if he was seeing double. Two Jarems stood facing Ayva. They were the same except for their clothes and something weird about the eyes of one of them.

"His name is Fenn," Jarem said. "He's my twin."

Tommis couldn't see Ayva's face, but he imagined the expression of shock and disbelief that must've filled it.

"How is this possible?" Her voice trembled.

"I've been in hiding all my life," Fenn said. "No one knows I'm alive." He sounded like Jarem, though not quite the same. His tone carried a sarcastic edge with a bitter undercurrent.

"Why?"

"I'm blind."

Ayva clapped her hands against her cheeks. "But... were you... were you born this way?"

Her question didn't require an answer. Why else would they have hidden him? Tommis held his breath to smother his own astonished reaction. It was unthinkable. Jarem's mother had kept a defective.

"Your mother didn't tell anyone? She broke the law?" Ayva said.

"She ignored it."

"What if the immortals find out?" she whispered.

"You know what they do to defectives," Fenn said. "And to anyone who stands up for them."

"Why did she do it? What was she thinking?"

"I guess she must've liked me. I'm not sure why."

"There's nothing else wrong with him. You'd be amazed what he can do. His other senses are much more developed than ours," Jarem said.

"You make me sound like a trick pony," the brother said.

"You know what I mean."

"Can you see anything at all?" Ayva said.

"Not a thing."

None of them spoke for a moment while Ayva struggled to absorb what they'd told her.

"Why are you telling me now, Jarem?" she asked.

"Because I trust you. Because I love Fenn. And if I'm picked at the Rite... I won't be able to help him anymore... not for years, anyway. He'll be stuck at home with no one but our mother to talk to. We thought maybe you could bring him outside once in a while."

"Take him out? What if we're seen?"

"Only after dark. And only to someplace that's sure to be deserted at night."

"My father would kill me if he found out."

"Or maybe you could just visit the house sometimes when our mother's not home," Fenn said. "Do you play chess?"

Ignoring his question, she said, "What if I'm also called into the immortals' service at the Rite?"

"Then I'm out of luck. We're all out of luck. But if you're not picked..." Fenn's voice held a hopeful tone. "I understand if you don't want to. If you were caught with me... I don't know what would happen. I probably shouldn't be asking you to take a risk like that. It's just, the thought of Jarem being gone scared me. Something could happen to my mother too, and then what? I guess... it's important to me that someone else knows I exist. You don't have to come. I already feel better just having shared my secret with you."

Because Tommis knew Ayva's strongest, most endearing and most annoying quality was the sympathy she always felt for other creatures, her response didn't surprise him.

"I'll come. Of course I will. I don't care about the danger. You're Jarem's brother. Fenn, right? I'll do what I can."

The blind brother reached out his hand, and she took it between hers. "My brother's a lucky bastard to end up with a treasure like you," he said.

"You can't tell anyone," Jarem said. "Not even your sister."

"I won't. Of course not. You don't have to worry about me."

"Thank you," Jarem said. "We should go now. Mother might wake and notice us missing."

After promising to work out the details of future visits

later, Ayva turned back the way she came, and the brothers took the cross path. They set off at a good clip, despite the blind one having to lean on the other for direction.

As Tommis emerged from his place of hiding, he recalled Aphrodite's words of encouragement. *Trust in the immortals.* Jarem's mother had broken one of their most sacred laws. It was up to him to do something about it.

14

CHARLET

Annoyingly, the boys were still not up by the time Charlet returned from checking the traps. She thought they had gone to bed early last night. Why they needed twelve plus hours of sleep was beyond her. She knocked hard on their bedroom door. "Time to wake up."

They straggled out from their room by the time she had sausage, eggs, and potatoes prepared for all of them. No one seemed in the mood for conversation. The boys ate fast, like always, and Fenn set to skinning the rabbits when he was done. Despite his lack of vision, he performed the job better and faster than his brother or her.

"You going to practice?" she asked Jarem.

"I guess."

"With the Rite almost here, you can't afford to miss it." Though the selection was supposed to be random, she suspected the immortals of cheating and making sure the youths most athletically inclined received the mark. If so, Jarem was bound to be a favorite pick. He needed to be as prepared as possible for the likelihood of his having to undergo the Trials.

He stood there looking at her like he was going to speak, before strapping on his sandals and heading out the door, saying nothing. She supposed a good mother would've tried to get him to share whatever was on his mind, but she figured it must be about his desire to escape the Rite, and as much as she might wish for the same thing, she could not give him any encouragement. He must take part in the ceremony, come what may.

Despite the deep challenges in her life—protecting Fenn from discovery being highest on this list—she had made it thus far by not dwelling on matters that weren't within her power to change. Keeping busy provided the best distraction, and therefore she began every morning with a thorough cleaning of their cottage.

But it wasn't long before Fenn called out to her from the kitchen. "Someone's coming this way on horseback."

She couldn't hear any sounds outside, but his ears were much better than hers. They weren't expecting visitors, and a surprise one was never good. Trying not to panic, she hurried to the window and peered out the front. Her breath caught in her throat at the sight of Apollo riding toward their house. *What in Skalbourne?* In the seconds it took for her to find her voice, he was already dismounting. "Hide!" she hissed at Fenn.

He knew better than to waste time asking questions. He dropped the knife on the counter and flew to his room, pulling the door shut behind him. Jarem had built a hiding place that he could crawl into from a built-in seat bench with a false bottom.

A firm knock landed on the door. Charlet held her breath, waiting for Fenn to have the chance to hide. She considered pretending no one was home. But he was an immortal; if no one answered, he had every right to force his way in, and then how would she explain why she ignored him?

As soon as the noises from Fenn's bedroom stopped, she opened the front door and bowed her head. "Welcome, my lord."

"Good morning." His voice reeked of arrogance.

But when she looked up, it struck her how his eyes seemed to see right into her. She had never met a more handsome man, though she could not have said which particular feature made him so. Despite her powerful feelings against him and his kind, her awareness of his physical presence—his height and his musculature—made her knees go weak. She had to balance herself with a hand on the table.

She cursed herself. *He's a ruthless immortal. He would strike you down in an instant if he knew what you had done.*

"How may I be of service?" She said in a curt tone. He had no business coming here, and she did not want to encourage him to stay.

"I believe it's customary in Skalbourne to invite visitors into your home."

Fury welled up inside her. It was bad enough they had control of the town, but at least her own house ought to be a place of refuge. She would've slammed the door in his smug face, if not for Fenn. For his sake, she must stifle her feelings and pretend to welcome Apollo's attention. She gritted her teeth and said, "You honor me too much," while stepping back to allow him entry. "I apologize for the bloody mess on my counter, my lord. I've been skinning rabbits." She hoped this would serve as a gentle reminder that he ought to send prior notice before visiting.

"You don't need to apologize," he said, oblivious to her subtext. His gaze swept the place as he strode in, looking tall and regal like the immortal he was.

She had not been with a man for many years. Only this could explain her sudden urge to feel Apollo's powerful arms holding her close. When he turned his piercing eyes on her, she lowered her own gaze so he wouldn't see her desire.

But when she looked again, he had shifted his glance toward Fenn's chessboard, resting on the shelf with all its pieces in place. Her stomach clenched. What if he noticed the pegs and the dark squares being higher than the white? How would she explain them? Fenn was supposed to put it back in his chest whenever he finished playing. But it was her fault too; she should've noticed it earlier. They had all grown complacent.

"Please, have a seat." She gestured at a chair that faced away from the shelf.

"I'd rather stand."

"As you wish." She knew she ought to provide him with refreshments, but that would only extend the visit. He needed to leave as soon as possible. If only he would get to the point. "I must admit, I can't help wondering what could've brought you here, my lord."

He turned back to the shelves and pulled out her book on human anatomy. His behavior disgusted her. Immortal or not, he ought to know it was common courtesy to ask for permission before pawing anyone's private possessions. After flipping through several of the sketches, he gave her a curious glance. "Are you a doctor?"

"I hope to become one someday."

When he restored the book to its place on the shelf, he looked at the chessboard again. "You play?"

"I'm not very good. May I offer you tea?" Anything to distract him, even if it slowed his departure.

He picked up the board and ran his hand over the uneven tiles. Pulling out a piece, he stared at the peg attached underneath it. "I've never seen anything like this."

"My son made it."

He rolled the piece in his hand. "Interesting. It's smooth except the top. Was that a mistake?"

Without waiting for her answer, he compared it to another black piece, and then to the white pieces. "Black are rough, white are smooth."

He was seconds away from figuring out why that might be. She had to say something. "Jarem made it for my father. He lost his vision in old age."

"I was just about to say the board is well-suited to a blind person. Your son must be very clever."

She said nothing, afraid that Jarem's intelligence might make him more likely to be chosen for the Trials.

Apollo replaced the board on the shelf. "Word has it you're one of the most skilled hunters in Skalbourne. Would you agree?"

"People are kind."

"Please, no modesty."

"I'm reasonably accomplished," she said.

"We need hunters in Olympus."

She stared at him in confusion. "I don't understand."

"Hunters. We have a shortage, currently, and a love of game meat. You would hunt deer and wild boar, primarily."

"Just me?"

"Of course not, there are others."

"I... I live here. I couldn't leave my son. I'm sure you can find someone else for the job."

He raised his eyebrows, looking incredulous that she

dared to refuse his command. She realized she must've sounded blunt, discourteous, and ungrateful for the honor of being singled out by an immortal. But this was no different than how she behaved during their previous encounter. If he'd paid the slightest bit of attention, he could've saved himself the trouble of this visit.

"Your son is sixteen, isn't he?" Apollo said.

That he knew so much about her gave her an icy feeling inside. "Yes."

"He might be chosen at the Rite. Then you would have nothing keeping you here."

"First, there is a very good chance he will not be chosen." *Especially if you do not make a point of it*, she wanted to add, but didn't dare. "Second, I have a life here in Skalbourne. Friends and occupations that fill my time."

"Have you ever seen Olympus?"

She shook her head.

"It's beautiful. You would live well there, much better than here." He looked around the house as if it were a dump. He was not helping his cause by doing so. "You would be compensated well. You could afford a luxurious home. Many mortals live happily in Olympus."

It was the last place she would want to be, but she knew it wouldn't do to offend Apollo. "You do me much honor, my lord. May I have time to consider your generous offer?"

He stiffened. "Of course."

When she saw him to the door, she noticed he had an ordinary horse tied to the post outside. "I trust your blest horse is in good health?" It might've been wiser not to ask, but when it came to the welfare of animals, she couldn't help herself.

"She's dead." His eyes clouded and all at once she felt a sameness between them. She'd never seen an immortal look so human before. Of course, it was widely known that they bonded closely with their horses.

Charlet itched to find out how the blest horse might've died, but she held herself back from asking. She did not want to deepen his pain by pushing him to talk about it. "My deepest condolences for your loss, my lord." Her sympathy was sincere.

"Thank you." He took a step down. "I'll return in a week to find out your decision."

She cursed under her breath after he'd gone out. Moving to the window, she remained watching until he spurred his horse. Then she hurried into the boys' bedroom. Decisions needed to be made. She was already calculating how quickly they could pack and move to another town in the north where, if they were lucky, the immortal wouldn't follow her.

15

FENN

Fenn heard the seat bench being lifted and Mother telling him to come out.

Thank the immortals. He hated the hiding place, which was not much wider or longer than a coffin. It might've been worse if he could see the confined space, but it was bad enough feeling the hard surface surrounding him. He reached up and turned the latch, raising the false bottom of the seat, before clambering out from there.

Mother was pacing. "Could you hear us?"

"Not much."

"It was Apollo."

He must've looked like he didn't believe her, because then she added, "Yes, the actual immortal. Jarem and I had the misfortune of running into his blest horse the other day. It was all a misunderstanding, and he accepted that, I thought. But the encounter must've brought me to his attention. According to him, they're in need of hunters in Olympus."

"What for?"

"Same reason as anyone else, I guess. They want to eat

fresh meat but don't have the skills or desire to hunt for it themselves."

"Why can't Zeus strike animals down with a lightning bolt or something?"

"Oh they love to give us reasons to work for them. They believe that if they use their powers to take care of everything, we'll have never have any incentive to leave our beds."

"Do you think that's true?"

"Of course not. I think the immortals are lazy and love having mortals do all the actual work. But this is neither here nor there. He's commanded me to help him. It doesn't matter what I think. And we have a more immediate problem. He saw your chess set."

Fenn's heart sank. "I'm an idiot."

"What's done is done. You've been preoccupied too."

"Did he get why it was designed like that?"

"Yes. I told him Jarem made it for my father after he lost his sight in old age. But what if he checks the town register? He could find out your grandfather died when Jarem was three."

"Why do you think he wouldn't believe you?"

"I don't know. Maybe he did believe me. But we can't take the chance. We need to hide you for a while. In case he gets suspicious about who exactly is blind in our household, and he comes back to search."

Sweat dampened his forehead at the thought of going back into that coffin-like box. "I can't stay there for more than an hour. You don't know what it's like."

She cupped his cheek with her hand. "I wouldn't ask you to. We'll have to think of somewhere else. Or maybe even reconsider moving to another town sooner. When your brother comes home, we'll figure out what to do. In the meantime, please put your board away."

THE TRIALS

Fenn heard the sounds then. He would've noticed them sooner if the conversation had not distracted him. A horse whinnied in the distance, and heavy footfalls crunched the pine needles and gravel outside. "Someone's coming. Fast!" he shouted. Before he could turn and sprint back to his room, he heard the door bang open and boots stomp across the floor toward him. Muscular hands gripped him on both sides.

"Let go of us!" Mother shrieked, letting Fenn know they had her too.

Another set of footsteps entered the house, moving at a deliberate pace. Sweaty fingers grasped Fenn's chin and turned his face. The man's breath reeked of garlic.

"Leave him alone!" Mother shouted. "How dare you break into our house?"

"Look at these eyes," the man with the revolting breath mused. "Like a thick fog."

After all the years of hiding, his secret was out in a matter of seconds. It only took one person gazing upon him.

"Who sent you here?" Mother said.

"Under the laws of immortals and mortals, we are placing you and your son under arrest," the man told her.

She did not deny he was her son. There was no hope of pretending he was a friend or relation from out of town. One look at Fenn standing next to Jarem, and they would know the boys were twins.

"On what charge?" she asked, though the answer was obvious.

"The charge of failing to report a defective birth."

"He only went blind recently."

"Tell the council that. But I would not hold out hope of their believing you. I've seen your son Jarem, and he looks identical to this one, though his eyes are normal. There's no record of Jarem having a twin. This is clear evidence of intent to hide a defective birth."

"Let Fenn go. He's done nothing wrong. The crime, if any, is mine alone."

"Again, it's up to the council to decide what must be done with him."

Fenn tried to break away as the defenders moved him toward the door, but a swift kick in the back of the knee hobbled him. It must have been Apollo who sent them, he thought. It was his own fault for leaving out the chessboard. He knew he ought to be feeling an array of emotions, from guilt, to anger at his captors, to fear of whatever they planned to do with Mother and him.

Instead, with the crushing burden of his secret existence dissolved, a glorious and unexpected sensation of lightness filled him.

16

I, ASTERIOS

Moros startled me out of a beautiful dream. I had been lying on the ground with Helena's mother beside me, resting her head against my long neck. We were alone in a lush garden, with no pesky intruders, mortal or otherwise. I heard what I thought was young Helena scampering beside us, but when I looked, I saw a colt instead. Though the time and place made no sense, I was certain this was my new grandson. My heart was near to bursting when the dream ended.

"Asterios!" As Moros pulled on my mane, I was as close as I'd ever come to biting him, but somehow I restrained myself.

"Where's your saddle?" He spun back around to search my stall, as if it would be in here. But even if I thought he would understand me, I would not have deigned to answer him.

Moros was a mess. He was wearing his pajamas and slippers, which were steeped in mud. His thin gray hair stuck out in patches and his face had a long scratch on one side.

When he turned, I noticed a tear on the back of his pajama leg.

"Where's your saddle?" he said again without expectation of an answer. He left the stall to check other parts of the stable, making a commotion that woke other blest horses. Ismene peered over the wall separating us and I gave her a *don't blame me* toss of my head.

Before long, Moros found my customary saddle and brought me outside. I had no wish to carry him anywhere at this time of night, but when you have been bonded with a particular immortal since birth, you lack the power to resist any of his commands.

Moros, who had grown weak in recent years, struggled to put on my halter and saddle, a chore that was always performed by stable hands. I did not understand why Moros had not rousted one up, since they slept in the dormitory mere yards from where we were. "We must find Henry," he kept babbling. "We must save the boy."

I had my doubts that Moros could tolerate a ride all the way to Skalbourne. His fingers struggled with the saddle buckles. He kept glancing back toward the Palace of Olympus like he was fearful of who or what might emerge from there. Given his urgency to get away, I wondered if the other immortals had been holding him against his will. They almost never imprisoned one of their own, though I had heard of cases occurring many years ago, during the Dark Age. Immortals were so accustomed to lording over everyone, they lashed out against Zeus's tight governance of them on rare occasion.

"He took my medallion and now Zeus is furious," Moros muttered. "He's just a boy! Boys do stupid things sometimes. I'm sure he meant to give it back."

I was equally certain he did not mean to give it back.

"I'll straighten things out when we find him. He'll return the medallion and apologize, and then we can forget about all this nonsense." Moros finished securing the saddle and tried to clamber onto me, but he was used to a stable hand helping him and could not, on his own, raise his leg high enough. He slid backward. "Stay still, Asterios!"

If I stood any stiller, I'd be a statue.

He tried again, with the same results. But the third time, after throwing his chest forward and scrabbling up like a lizard, he settled into the saddle. "Go!" he shouted.

I took measured steps because I knew he would fall off if I cantered.

"Faster!" He whipped me with the riding crop.

That was asking for it. I launched myself toward the road and he tilted sideways, barely holding on. "Slow down!" he cried out, just as a thunder of hooves approached from behind. I glanced back to see five or six defenders on horseback, with Ares atop Petros at the lead. "Halt!" Ares called out.

Straightening himself, Moros wielded the riding crop again and again. He dug in his heels and I whinnied in protest as Ares closed in on us. "Faster!" my immortal master shouted again, but instead I slowed, despite his command, because his safety was my primary concern and it was clear he would lose his grip if I obeyed him.

Ares and the defenders surrounded us, forcing me to stop.

"Leave me alone, Ares! This is none of your business," Moros said.

"Get off your horse or I'll have my men take you down!"

The defenders exchanged glances, clearly uncomfortable with the possibility of having to lay hands on Moros.

They weren't ever supposed to touch immortals, let alone subdue them.

But Moros, recognizing an impossible situation, dismounted himself.

"Zeus ordered you to remain in your apartments," Ares said.

"I wanted fresh air. How dare you stop me?"

"Who did you bribe to unlock the door for you?"

"What have you done with Henry?" Moros said.

I wondered why they continued to waste their breath on questions that were not getting answered.

"Henry? You mean Belic?"

"I mean my son!"

Ares drew up in fury. He spat out to his men: "Take Moros back to his apartments and remain on watch outside his door."

"If you harm a hair on that boy's head, you'll feel my wrath," Moros said.

"*Your* wrath?!" Ares leapt down from Petros and drew out his sword in one well-practiced movement. Looming over Moros, he grabbed his arm, wrenched it behind his back, and placed the blade against his neck.

Though he was immortal, Moros trembled.

"You will do as I say." Ares lowered the sword and thrust Moros toward the defenders, who caught him before he could fall. Moros yanked his arms away from them, brushed himself off, and set off toward the palace with the defenders following close on his heel.

A stable hand was called to return me to my stall. I wished I could return to my dream, but I had much to worry about now. I did not think Ares would make the mistake twice of allowing Moros to escape. I might never see my master again. I would not put it past the immortals to keep one of their own imprisoned for eternity.

Though I wanted to believe the immortals were never-changing, I could not deny the evidence of my eyes and ears. Moros, who had been sharp as a tack, was now as confused as a mortal man in his dotage. He thought Belic was his son? I had never heard of any immortals having mortal offspring.

Physical deterioration was also evident. There had been a time when he mounted the saddle with ease. He could ride for days and walk for hours. But now he struggled for breath following the mildest exertion.

He had always looked like the oldest of the immortals, and now he acted like it. It made me wonder if perhaps they felt the effects of aging, only at a far more gradual pace than mere mortals.

It grieved me to imagine the immortals growing older and weaker. I had served Moros with pride. Death would likely come to me within several years—I had already reached an age that few other blest horses attained. Still, I was a noble steed that could walk the lands with head held high. But what did it mean when the noblest animal in Hellas served a weak master?

17

TOMMIS

Tommis had known what must be done when he returned home after following Ayva. Slinking into the front room, he had found a piece of crumpled blank paper and an old stub of a pencil in a drawer. He had spread the paper in front of him on a flat rock outside, and with as few words as possible, he had accused the Woodgard mother of giving birth to a defective twin and hiding him at her house for the last sixteen years. Afterward, Tommis had run all the way to Council Hall to slide his anonymous note under the door. Dawn was breaking by the time he returned and crept onto his mattress, falling almost instantly asleep.

It was past mid-day when he opened his eyes again. Lucky for him, Pa had grudgingly agreed to repair someone's roof and had left early after gathering his tools, neglecting to wake Tommis like usual. Work didn't come often to Pa anymore, not with his reputation for drinking, so he felt obliged to take the few jobs that were offered. He despised physical labor, but it was always a good excuse for drowning himself in liquor and torturing Tommis and Ma at the end of the day.

Even if Tommis caught every rat in town today, Pa would still be ready to belt him when he returned in the evening. So instead of hurrying off to work, he lay in bed a while longer, mulling over what he'd done last night. It bothered him a little that Jarem's mother and brother would most likely be hung for their crimes. However, it was a very clear cut case of her breaking the law, and as the defender he hoped to become, he would need to steel himself against feeling sympathy for transgressors. Soon enough, if all went as he hoped, he would be spending his days tracking down and apprehending lawbreakers of all types.

As for Jarem's brother, he could hardly be blamed for the crime since he was an infant when the decision was made to save him. But the fact remained he was a defective, and the immortals in their wisdom had dictated their removal. It was well known that mortals inherited characteristics from their parents, and that if defectives were allowed to grow up and have children of their own, those defective characteristics would weaken the population of mortals until they became so susceptible to disease a single outbreak might wipe them all out. This had happened during the Dark Age, according to the Book of the Immortals.

A desire to remove Jarem as a rival for Ayva's affection was not part of his motivation. He didn't know whether Jarem would be held responsible for any part of the deception regarding his brother, but even if he were to be hanged, it would not change Tommis's burning desire to join the defenders and rise within the ranks in a way that would attract the approval of the immortals. Besides, Ayva was not destined to become the wife of any mortal. His conviction that she would be chosen to be blest grew with each passing day.

Tommis had considered signing his name to the note, in the hope of pleasing Aphrodite if she were to learn of it. But he had to be careful; he wasn't a defender yet. Someone might question how he found out about Jarem's brother, and if maybe he had known about the blind boy for some time without telling anyone. They might consider him guilty by association. It was best not to take the chance, and to hope for an opportunity to reveal his role in the arrest to Aphrodite later on.

Satisfied he'd made the right choices, Tommis moved on to more urgent considerations. He imagined several scenarios for how to get himself picked at the Rite. One thought was simply to ply Pa with liquor on the morning of the event. If he was passed out at home, he wouldn't be able to stand in Tommis's way.

But Pa was too sly for this. Many times in the past, he had held off drinking when it meant he would have the chance to crush the hopes and dreams of another person. Usually that person was Tommis or Ma, though other friends and family members sometimes fell prey to Pa's wickedness too.

What if Tommis left matters to chance? *Chance is for the weak*, according to Aphrodite. Maybe it could be a mixture of chance and intention. From what he'd heard, most sixteen-year-olds prayed not to be chosen. He could stand beside one of the reluctant ones. Then, if that person received the mark, he would slyly switch it with his own blank paper. The other boy or girl would cooperate to save themselves from the Trials.

The plan still left too much to chance. Pa would watch him like a hawk, and would be the first to cry foul if he saw his son doing a swap. Or if Pa somehow missed it, an official, or worse yet, an immortal, might have their eyes on him. The last thing he wanted to do was anger the immortals.

The third option was closer to what Aphrodite appeared to suggest. *Only one thing blocks you. Remove it.* Of course she didn't mean that he should kill Pa. There were other methods of getting someone out of the way for a while. Like making them sick.

The thing about being a ratcatcher was how everyone considered it normal if you had arsenic scattered around the house. A colorless, tasteless poison was always an accident waiting to happen, or at least should appear that way to others. A ratcatcher knew the relative doses that might sicken or kill an animal or a person.

When he recovered, Pa would guess who was behind his bout of nausea. By then, it would be too late. The Rite would be over. Those selected were always taken away immediately to prepare for the Trials. There would be no turning back.

After Tommis finished his oatmeal, at Ma's request, he joined her in the garden to help with the weeding. He pondered how to feed the arsenic to his father while making sure his mother ate none of it, until Ma moved closer and spoke to him.

"Is it important to you, Tommis? I mean, taking the Rite to become a defender?"

"Ma... I wanted this all my life. Not just to get away from..." he nodded toward the house. "I want to serve the immortals. You know how they say, if you serve them well enough, you can become one of them? I dream about that. I know I'm nothing but a ratcatcher, but that's not supposed to matter."

"We're humble folk. Do you really think it's possible for people like us?"

"It doesn't matter what your birth is. It's your devotion that matters. Your willingness to serve and protect. Your desire to bow to the immortals' will."

"I suppose. That's what they say."

"Would you give me your permission to volunteer?" he asked, wanting to be certain that if Pa was out of the way, Ma would not interfere on his behalf.

"I would. But not him. Not ever." She ventured a frightened glance toward the back room where he was to be found most of the time.

"Do you think you could change his mind?"

"When have I ever done that?"

He couldn't think of a time. "Why do you stay with him? Why didn't you leave years ago?"

"You know why. He would find me and kill me. Worse, he'd kill you too, probably first, just to torture me."

"So you're just going to live like this until one of you dies?"

She shrugged. "Maybe I don't have it in me to oppose him."

"Then I just have to give up on my dreams."

She flinched and lowered her eyes before attacking a prickly weed with her spade.

18

AYVA

Ayva returned home in the heat of mid-afternoon after gathering blackberries for a pie. Rennie had said she was going to get them, and now she was nowhere to be found. Poppa was at work. Sometimes she felt they took advantage of her good nature. It was bad enough she was expected to cook everything the family ate, but now she had to fetch the ingredients too. If she did get picked at the Rite, they were going to be in for a rude awakening when they finally had to do a few things for themselves.

To make matters worse, the coal bucket in the kitchen lay empty. Another job Rennie was supposed to do. Now Ayva had to go all the way out to the shed to fetch more, and her skirt would probably get filthy in the process.

If she were anyone else, she would allow them to come home to cold food and nothing for dessert. But she couldn't bring herself to neglect them. As foul a mood as she might be in right now, it would only upset her more to see the disappointment in their faces at having to scrounge in the pantry for dried meats and nuts and stale bread.

She snatched the coal bucket and tromped out the back door toward the shed. Couldn't they have built it closer to the house? But father had said it was wisest to keep anything that burned easily, like coal and firewood, as far from their home as possible.

Stomping her way right up to the door, she set down the bucket to click open the latch. To her astonishment, a small horse leapt at her the second the door came open. She screamed, falling backward, while it leaned over her and licked her arm. Its tongue tickled her, which made her laugh as she pulled herself into a sitting position. "How did you get here?" She pet its forelocks. This was when she noticed the beginnings of a horn growing on the bridge of its nose.

Oh my immortals. She scrambled backwards away from it, but the horse followed and gave her a little nudge like it wanted to play. "Go away!" she shouted. It was forbidden to touch a blest horse, but what if they touched *you*?

"Xander!" Rennie called out. "Xander, leave her alone!"

Now the little horse scampered to Rennie, who hugged her head and pressed her close. Ayva couldn't believe her eyes.

"Let me explain," Rennie said.

Ayva pulled herself up. "Rennie, you're insane. What are you doing? Where did this blest foal come from? Did you steal it? What are we going to do with it? They're going to kill you. The immortals will kill you for this."

Rennie lowered the bucket of milk she had been carrying, and let the horse drink from it. "It wasn't my fault. I came upon his dead mother in the forest. Apollo's blest horse."

"Apollo?! Zeus help us."

"At first no one was around, except her little colt. I

named him Xander. He licked up some blackberries I picked for you. Then I heard Apollo coming with some defenders. I hid, of course. I couldn't let them catch me standing there next to his dead horse. But when I hid, Xander came after me. I held him to keep him silent, and then... well, he probably thinks I'm his mother now. What could I do? I brought him back here."

"What could you do? Leave him there, that's what."

"He followed me."

"You fed him blackberries!"

"I didn't mean to."

"And now milk!"

"I can't let him starve, poor little thing. He needs me. I bring him goats' milk."

"What do you think is going to happen when he gets bigger? Soon he won't even fit inside this shed. What then?" Ayva was beside herself. Rennie had never had good judgment, but this was beyond everything. She was going to get the whole family executed.

"I know, I know. I'm just trying to keep him alive till he can eat on his own. Then I can release him someplace where the immortals will find him. Obviously I'm not planning to keep him forever."

"It's not at all obvious what you're planning to do. It doesn't seem like you've given this any thought at all. Putting a blest horse in our shed. He could've hurt me!"

Rennie actually laughed. "Oh please. The horn's just a stub. And I saw him greet you. He's like a friendly puppy. He'll kill you with licks if you're not careful."

"There's nothing funny about this. You need to give that horse back now."

Xander looked at Rennie, then continued drinking as she pet his flank.

"You must bring him to the temple tonight and tie him there," Ayva said. "A defender will find him in the morning and tell the immortals."

"Tie him up? What if some larger creature attacks and he can't run away?"

"He's bigger than most other animals already. They'll leave him alone."

"He might freeze during the night."

"Fine. We'll bring him right before dawn. Then it won't be long before someone comes and sees him."

Rennie made a face. "All right. I guess I don't have a choice."

But watching the adoring way Xander gazed at her sister, even Ayva felt a pang of regret for what they would have to do.

19

JAREM

It surprised Jarem to find the front door ajar on his return from practice. Normally, it was locked as protection against anyone wandering in and catching Fenn off guard. Now and then one of them would forget, naturally. They were probably both in their rooms and didn't hear the wind pushing the door open.

"Mother?" Jarem called out. He had practiced for hours, working up an appetite, and then had gotten an enormous meal in town with a few friends. He wanted to let her know he wouldn't be hungry for supper.

Her door was partway open, and when she didn't reply, he looked in to find her room empty.

"Fenn?" Jarem got an unsettled feeling inside when no response came from his brother either. "Where the hades is everyone?" He looked in the bedroom he shared with Fenn and that, too, was empty.

Fenn rarely went out during daylight hours. He almost never stepped outside without Jarem first checking to make sure the coast was clear.

Jarem looked out the back window but couldn't see

either of them behind the house. He wondered then if his brother might've gone into hiding and fallen asleep in there. He raised the seat bench, but once again, no Fenn.

Maybe Mother had needed him for a job outside, like lifting something heavy, that couldn't wait till Jarem's return. Or maybe something had happened to their mother out there, and she'd screamed for help, and Fenn was now rushing to her rescue. He hurried out the back door and circled the house repeatedly, peering through the woods, listening for voices, and making a wider arc each time around. Still nothing. He didn't dare say Fenn's name in case anyone else heard him, but he continuously called out for their mother. *Where were they?* He couldn't imagine Fenn ever wandering beyond shouting range of their home. Unless he got lost.

Dread prickled inside him. Something was wrong. He returned inside and looked for signs of intruders that might have come to rob or attack them. But nothing was bloodied or knocked over. On examining closer, he noticed more dirt on the floor near the front door than was normal. And there was also the fact that someone had left it open.

It occurred to him Mother might be out running errands, and Fenn could've gone missing since she left. He set out for town and spent the next hour wandering through shops and asking people if they'd seen her. No one had.

Late in the day he turned his steps homeward, following a different route than before. Passing on the opposite side of the guardhouse, he noticed a beggar woman staring hard at him. He stopped to give her a few pennies.

"I seen you before," she said. "Looked like you couldn't see nothin'."

He froze in place. "Where was I going?"

"Defenders had you. Took you outta their coach and

dragged you in there." She nodded at the guardhouse. "You don't remember?"

"No."

"There were a woman with them too. Older. Your mother, might be?"

His head spun. Weakness overcame him, and he stumbled to the ground beside the beggar woman. He lowered his head over his knees, feeling like weeping, but the tears wouldn't come. Everything was over. Defenders must've come to their house and arrested his mother and Fenn.

He should never have agreed to tell Ayva. Sixteen years of keeping the secret, and the day after he tells someone, they're found out. He didn't believe she turned them in, but maybe she told her sister Rennie, and she told someone else, and then it reached a person who didn't care what happened to his family. Or maybe Ayva's father caught her returning home late and forced the truth from her. No matter how the secret got out, it was his fault. He shouldn't have let Fenn talk him into it.

"Don't go there," the beggar woman said, seeing his eyes on the guardhouse. "If they take you again, you won't never get out."

His legs wobbled and the thought of seeing his loved ones restrained inside a dank, miserable cell turned his stomach. But he needed to talk to them if he could. He forced himself to his feet and staggered across the road.

Two defenders flanked the front entrance. They said nothing and continued staring straight ahead as he grasped the iron ring and yanked open the ponderous wooden door. He entered a domed hall, mostly empty except for a small, tired official seated behind a bulky desk. An imposing metal gate, watched by two more guards, blocked access to the rest of the building.

"State your business." The man's voice echoed loudly.

"I want to know if my mother was brought here. Charlet Woodgard."

The official riffled through a pile of papers on his desk. "Hmm. Yes, admitted today at noon. Along with her son, I guess that would be your brother, name of Fenn."

"I'd like to see them."

"Not allowed."

"Why not?"

"No visitors until their case is reviewed by the council."

"When will that be?"

"Don't know."

"How long does it usually take?"

"Could be a week. Could be months."

"I'm sixteen years old. I need to speak with them before the Rite."

"There are no exceptions to the rules."

Jarem was wasting his time here; this man had no authority. He needed to speak to someone who did.

Darkness had set in by the time he reached Ayva's house. Through the lit window, he saw her in the kitchen, placing dishes on the counter. He was about to go to the door when her father walked into view. *Shit.* He needed to talk to her privately first. Without accusing her of anything, he wanted to find out how much the authorities knew about Fenn. She could advise him on the best way to appeal to the council through her father. Though patience was difficult, he would be in a better position if he waited till her father left for work in the morning. With her help, and her father's, they might save his family yet.

20

AYVA

Rennie, who was at least always true to her word, woke at three in the morning and got Ayva up. Poppa was a deep sleeper, fortunately. His snoring continued above the sound of their footsteps across the floor, and the opening and closing of the back door.

Xander pranced up and down with excitement when they reached the shed. "He'll need one more feeding." Rennie supplied his milk while Ayva waited with impatience.

"At least we have moonlight to guide us tonight," Rennie said, softening Ayva with her optimism.

After Xander slurped all the milk, Rennie attached a lead to his neck and shoulders. He didn't mind being led by her, though he did frequently try to pull her in another direction. Imagine how it would be when he realized his strength was greater than hers.

They followed the path behind their house that connected to Gnarl Wood's network of trails. The sisters walked in silence, with Ayva just wanting to get the task done right away, and Rennie sulking about needing to give up a horse that never belonged to her in the first place.

Thin clouds spread across the sky, creating a shroud that reduced the moon's light to a dim glow. They approached the temple from the back, keeping themselves hidden behind trees, wary of defenders who might be watching the place. As they came around the building, Ayva's eyes shifted to the marble statue of Zeus.

A hooded figure was bent over the wide base of the statue.

"Rennie, stop!" she hissed, throwing out her arm to pause her sister.

They stood rooted in mingled terror and fascination. As the hooded man moved—she was certain from his size that he must be male—Ayva saw another form lying beneath him. She could tell from the bare legs, this one was female. The woman neither moved nor spoke.

Xander chuffed, causing Ayva's heart to skip a beat. Rennie slapped her hand over the horse's mouth. "Quiet," she whispered into his ear.

When the figure raised his head and they saw it was an immortal, not a man, Ayva gasped. Most terrifying of all was the red liquid—it had to be blood—that dripped from his lips and chin. He wiped it off with the back of his hand as he peered into the forest toward them. Her whole body trembled.

"Ares." Rennie mouthed the words.

He had a sharp nose, a cruel mouth, and rage-filled eyes. Ayva was certain if he discovered them, their deaths would be slow and torturous. He stood and took a step in their direction.

Rennie grabbed her sleeve, ready to run. But Ayva's feet

were rooted in place, almost as if the immortal was sending them a silent command to stay put.

The sound of horses came from the other direction. Ares turned as a group of five defenders rode up.

The captain dismounted and bowed his head before the immortal. "My lord, what is your command?" he said.

"Do you know this woman?" Ares spoke in a thunderous tone that caused the captain to flinch.

The captain moved closer. "Yes, my lord. Her name is Ginna Kleg. She recently gave birth to a defective and was very combative when we came to take the child away."

"Look at the knife. Do you think she would take her own life?"

"She was that distraught, yes, my lord."

Ares stepped down to the plaza. "Remove her from here and clean up before morning. No one can be allowed to see the statue debased."

As Ares moved away from them toward the stable where his blest horse no doubt awaited him, Rennie yanked Ayva's sleeve. Together, they crept back to the path. Xander clung to Rennie's other side, seemingly as eager to escape Ares' notice as the sisters were.

When they were out of earshot, they broke into a run and kept up the pace all the way home. It wasn't until Xander was safely in the shed that they spoke about what they had just seen.

Bile burned in the back of Ayva's throat. "It was Ginna, wasn't it? Our Ginna."

Rennie turned to her with features pinched in anger. "I saw her after the Welcoming. Her baby was deemed defective. She was beside herself with grief. Damn the immortals. Damn them to Hades and back."

"You think she really would've killed herself?"

"She could've... the way she was when I saw her. But Ares..." Her eyes widened in horror.

Ayva's stomach hardened at the memory of the blood on his face.

"What was he doing?" Rennie said.

"Don't think about it! It couldn't be real. We must've imagined it. Ginna killed herself. That's bad enough."

"It *was* real, but you're right we can't talk about it. We'll be dead faster than we can blink if the immortals or their minions hear what we saw."

The first light of dawn softened the sky. Ayva glanced toward the shed. "We'll deal with Xander later." The thought brought her no relief.

21

JAREM

Jarem refused to give in to despair regarding the fate of his mother and Fenn. There was no point in going to bed, because lying there unable to sleep would only encourage his mind to wander down gloomy paths. Instead, he resolved to work on a project he'd been meaning to accomplish well before the Rite, but had kept putting off for no good reason other than laziness.

Outside, he secured a heavy metal cup to a flat branch of the big, old oak near the back of the house. He left a small gap between the cup and the tree trunk for inserting the stick he had picked out a week ago. The freshly fallen maple branch had caught his eye for being sufficiently straight and of the right thickness.

He built a fire in the pit, and when it was hot enough, he placed one end of the maple branch on top of the flames. Though he'd never done this before, he'd watched Mr. Halloway demonstrate the process several times. He waited until the bark turned black, but not long enough for the fire to burn any deeper. The purpose was only to soften the wood, making it possible for him to bend it. Removing it from the flames, he inserted the burnt end between the metal cup and the trunk. With studied movements, he bent the stick by leveraging it around the cup and against the hard surface of the tree, over and over. When it was ready, he tied the rounded end of the stick to the straight part, forming a crook.

Sitting by the fire, he peeled off the blackened bark, exposing the clear, smooth wood underneath. He sat for some time, scraping off the rest of the bark and smoothing out any knots that remained. When he finished, he gazed at his creation with satisfaction.

It was a walking stick with a crook handle for Fenn. With his blindness no longer a secret, Fenn would need a cane to venture beyond the confines of their house after they released him from the guardhouse. Jarem refused to consider there might be any other outcome.

Shortly after dawn, he ate a quick meal and then set out for Ayva's house. There he leaned behind a large tree for an hour until her father left on the carriage that fetched him every morning. As soon as he was out of sight, Jarem hurried to the door and knocked lightly.

He didn't wait long before letting himself in. "Ayva?" he said. *Why was she still not up?* Normally she rose early, along with her sister. Both of their bedroom doors were closed. He slipped into Ayva's room to find her sleeping like the angel she was. Her face looked so peaceful, he wished he didn't have to disturb her with his awful news, but the lives of his mother and brother lay in the balance.

Her eyes snapped open in alarm when he touched her, but she calmed on recognizing him. "Is everything all right?" she asked.

"Your father said nothing last night?"

She shook her head. "No. What is it?"

"My mother... and Fenn... they've been arrested. They're being held at the guardhouse."

She pulled herself up. "What? No. That's impossible. How could they...?" She looked at him with sudden awareness. "You can't think I did this. I didn't tell a soul. I swear it."

"Are you sure? Not even Rennie?"

"I'm positive. Not even her. No one."

He had to believe her. She'd never lied to him before. Yet, it seemed like there must be a connection. The first time they told someone... and then this. "All right," he said. Now was not the time to make accusations. "Maybe someone saw Fenn and me when I brought him out the other night. I don't know. We can't change what happened. But maybe the council can go easy on them. It's been so many years. How could Fenn be a threat to anyone at this point? What good would it serve to punish them?"

"I can't imagine."

"I need to talk to your father. Can we go there together? He can help us, I'm sure."

Ayva's look was not so certain. "My father...?"

"Don't you think he'll do something? For his daughter's sake, if nothing else?"

"I don't know."

"At least we have to try."

"All right. Of course. " She stood up. "I need to get dressed."

Thankfully, Ayva's sister still had not risen by the time they left. She would've wanted to know what was happening, and any explanations would've delayed their departure. Besides, it was a struggle to speak openly about Fenn after so many years keeping his existence secret.

On their way to Council Hall, they discussed how they

would broach the topic with her father. Ayva advised him to let her handle the conversation as much as possible. As she predicted, her poppa greeted them with annoyance when they entered his office. "What are you two doing here? Never mind, I can guess."

Jarem stood at a distance while Ayva hastened to kiss her father, hoping to soften him. "Dear Poppa, Jarem's family needs our help."

"Don't *dear Poppa* me. There's nothing I can do."

"But you're head of the council."

"Jarem's mother broke the law. She deceived the immortals in order to keep a defective child."

"But Fenn has been hidden from view all his life. He's never hurt anyone or anything. It was as if he didn't exist. So where was the harm in my mother keeping him alive?"

"The law is clear on this. Her life will be forfeited. At least, that will almost certainly happen once she receives a full hearing."

"Poppa!" Tears sprang to Ayva's eyes. It took all Jarem's restraint to remain quiet.

"Can't you make an exception?" she pleaded. "In your position... can you ask the council to show mercy? Maybe a mild sentence, a slap on the wrist, would be good enough. It's just wrong to insist on taking her life for loving her child too much."

He patted her hand. "I sympathize," her father said. "I know how soft-hearted you are. But do you think she's the only parent impacted by the laws governing defectives? Nearly everyone I know has been affected. And when a child was born to them that wasn't whole and perfect, I'm sure they would've liked to keep it as well. The difference between them and Jarem's mother is they didn't act on their feelings and instincts. They acted according to the law."

"But Poppa..."

"Let me finish. They acted according to the law. How do you think they would feel if Mrs. Woodgard were to get away with flaunting that law? They would naturally think, I obeyed the law and my child was taken from me. Charlet Woodgard broke the law, got to keep her child, and suffered no consequences. There would be a revolt, you know. Many people would be angry and would rally against the unfairness of it all."

"Poppa, I think--," Ayva said.

"I'm not done. Not only that, but no one would ever obey the law again. 'No, you can't take my child who's missing a toe or a hand or half of his head. Charlet Woodgard got to keep her baby that had no eyes. No working eyes. Therefore I may keep mine too.' This is what everyone would say from now on."

"But couldn't mercy be shown in this one instance? Surely most people would be in favor of mercy?"

"As a general concept, I suppose. In practice, when it represents unfairness to others, then no, absolutely not."

"Sir," Jarem said. "Would it be possible to appeal directly to the immortals themselves?"

Councilman Tallis stared at him. "When it is a clear case of a law being broken... and when the punishment for said violation is also clearly defined... the immortals will not intervene. They never have during my lifetime, and never will. Appeals to the immortals, which rarely happen, are strictly reserved for situations that contain some ambiguity. This one most definitely does not."

"And what about my brother, sir? He committed no crime."

"Remaining in hiding once he was old enough to know he owed his existence to a criminal act could be considered no different from the crime committed by your mother. The same can be said of you, Jarem, for helping to keep him hidden."

"But we were children! We didn't know what we were doing."

"If you weren't aware of the consequences of your brother being found out, why did you hide him so effectively? That alone is evidence of intent to break the law."

"We did it out of love. Is that so terrible?"

"It's no excuse."

"I beg you to use your influence to spare the lives of my mother and brother."

"Please, Poppa." Ayva wiped tears from her cheeks.

"It would be improper for me to be influenced by the connection you have to my daughter. I would argue that a blind person has no way of functioning in our society and it would be a mercy to humanely return him to his makers."

Heat rushed through Jarem. If he'd had his knife with him, he would've been tempted to thrust it into the place where Tallis's heart should've been. Instead, he spun around and rushed from the room.

"Jarem!" Ayva said. "Poppa, how could you?!"

Jarem heard her footsteps behind him. "Wait for me!" she called out.

He quickened his pace, knowing he was being unreasonable, but unable to prevent his fury from spreading outward like an ever-widening cloud, encompassing not just her and her merciless father, but also the children who temporarily blocked his path in the road and their mother who attempted to speak to him. From there, he pictured the dark essence of his rage expanding across Skalbourne and beyond to Olympus, where it would lower over mortals and immortals alike and smother them all.

22

RENNIE

On waking late in the morning, Rennie was surprised to find both Poppa and Ayva had left without her hearing them. The sensation of viewing Ares in the midst of that unspeakable act must've exhausted her, because she'd fallen asleep so quickly she couldn't even remember getting into bed. Now, in the full light of morning, the events of last night all seemed like a terrible nightmare. At least she would try to view them that way, because the implications of what she'd seen were too ghastly to contemplate.

She hoped her anger and disgust would subside into a calmer awareness of the injustices they all faced, and that she would never allow herself to grow complacent about them.

But she wished Ayva had woken her when she got up. The open air market where Rennie hoped to find the man called Rhomer began early every morning and had no set closing time. Vendors left whenever they sold out their supply of goods. Now would be her only chance to secure this man's help. *The Rite was tomorrow.* The day had snuck up on them faster than she could have imagined.

Xander had to be fed before she could go, of course. He was excited to see her as always, especially since she gave him a special treat of berries after his milk. The colt wasn't yet ready to eat hay, but he managed fruit just fine. She wished she had time to take him out for exercise. Rennie had taught him to play fetch using a dish towel tied into a ball, and he loved chasing it as much as a dog would. But playing would have to wait till after dark. When she told him this, she got the sense he understood her. It had been the same way last night, when she'd whispered in his ear for him to be quiet. He hadn't made a peep after that. Blest horses were known for their intelligence, and maybe Xander possessed even more than the average amount.

On her way to the market, Verna, a friend of Ayva's who Rennie disliked, waved wildly and crossed the road toward her. The girl never stopped talking, and she didn't have time for it today, if she ever did. She was about to make an excuse to hurry away when Verna said, "How is Ayva? I couldn't believe it when I found out."

Found out what? Annoyed, Rennie paused to speak with her. "Ayva's fine," she said, because if Ayva wasn't fine, she ought to be the first to know.

"Isn't she worried about Jarem? What's going to happen to his family?"

The conversation was not making any sense. "His mother was well last I heard." She was all the *family* Jarem had, so far as she was aware.

"You don't know? She's in the guardhouse! Along with his secret twin brother, who's blind, as it turns out. I heard his eyes look spooky. So strange!"

Rennie gaped in disbelief. "You must be thinking of someone else. Jarem doesn't have a brother."

"They kept him hidden. Because he was blind, of course. Blind from birth. Mrs. Woodgard wasn't supposed to keep him."

Oh immortals. It was starting to seem possible. She recalled Ayva telling her no one ever went to his house because his mother was a sort of hermit and didn't like to be around people. Maybe this was why Ayva had gone out early this morning. She must've found out about it from someone.

"Where did you hear this?" Rennie asked.

"Our neighbor works at the guardhouse. He told my father. You can imagine our shock and surprise."

He ought to have kept his mouth shut, thought Rennie.

"He said they might arrest Jarem, too. You know, because he knew about it and helped hide him."

"He's not of age, though. I'm sure he was just doing what his mother told him to do," Rennie said.

"He's not a child. It was wrong what they did. I mean, hiding a defective. It's not fair. My best friend had her little brother taken, and he barely had anything wrong with him, not like being blind! Still, my friend's parents gave him up like you're supposed to."

"I have to run." Rennie had heard enough of Verna's opinions. Her head was spinning. She had always admired Mrs. Woodgard from a distance, and now she had even more respect for her. *The woman defied the immortals.* Rennie thought she would've done the same thing. And Jarem, too, protecting his brother. She had always viewed him as a bit of a dolt, but clearly he had a warm heart.

The news frightened Rennie, though. She could see how they all might end up paying for this crime at the hanging post. Maybe they hadn't arrested Jarem yet, but she suspected it was only a matter of time. This made it all the more urgent for both him and Ayva to run away before the Rite.

Rennie hurried to the market, which was set up in a wide field behind the meeting hall. Not wanting to attract attention, she pretended to be an interested buyer as she searched for the leather merchant. Her stomach fluttered at the sight of leather belts hanging from a rope suspended across two poles up ahead. But when she reached the stand, she found a woman seated behind the display. "Can I help you?" she said hopefully.

"Um, no thanks." Rennie continued to the next row of vendors. She was almost at the end when she spotted leather bags on a roughshod table. However, this time the seller was a very old man whose white beard fell almost to his waist. "Can I interest you in a pretty pouch to carry your coins?" he said.

Though he looked nothing like the loremaster's description, she said, "Your name isn't Rhomer, is it?"

"It could be, if that's what it will take to convince you that you'll never find better quality leather than mine." He picked up a handbag. "Feel this."

"No thanks. I don't suppose you've worked with someone of that name?"

"It's just me. I make the goods and I sell them. But maybe a belt would make a nice present for this fellow Rhoper."

If she didn't leave immediately, she would get stuck having to buy something. "Good day, sir."

With no other options, she returned to the woman selling belts and asked if she also worked alone.

"I don't make the leather. I was hired to manage this stall today," the woman said.

"Who hired you? Is his name Rhomer?"

She shook her head. "Hans."

Rennie turned to leave in disappointment, but then she paused. "Can you tell me what he looks like?"

"Oh, just your typical man. Medium height, medium weight. Brown hair. There's nothing remarkable about him."

This sounded exactly like what the loremaster had said. "When do you expect to see him?"

"He'll be back to collect his goods in the afternoon."

"What time?"

She shrugged. "He didn't say."

"When you see him, can you tell him Rennie would like to purchase something from him?"

"It's all here," she said.

"Something else. Tell him I'll be at the Tea House waiting." There was no place to linger at the market without being conspicuous. At the Tea House, she could sit at a little table out front and sip her tea all afternoon without attracting attention. She went directly there.

Three hours and what felt like a gallon of tea later, he still hadn't come. Rennie returned to the market only to find that all the vendors had packed up and left. She turned toward home with slumped shoulders.

After walking a short distance, she noticed a man on horseback passing her from the opposite direction. When he peered down at her, she thought he looked the way Rhomer and Hans had been described to her. Average height and weight, brown hair, no distinguishing marks. But just as she was about to speak to him, he flicked his reins and the horse cantered away.

23

RENNIE

Rennie heard Ayva crying through the closed door of her bedroom as soon as she entered the house. If only she had been able to return with hopeful news. "Ayva, let me in," she said on finding the door locked.

The weeping paused, but no sound of movement followed.

"Please, Ayva. We have to talk. Please let me help you."

After a few seconds, footsteps approached the door, and the bolt clicked open. Rennie threw her arms around her sister. "I heard what happened."

"It's even worse," Ayva said through tears. "Jarem and I went to Poppa's office this morning to plead his case."

Rennie knew without asking what the outcome must've been. "Oh immortals. Not even your sweet urging would ever get him to sway from a strict interpretation of the law."

"I... I thought maybe... I mean, he knows how important Jarem is to me... I thought maybe he would make an exception for once in his life. I'm a fool."

"You're not. You're kind and sympathetic and exactly what a good person should be."

"He's hateful." Ayva threw herself down on the bed.

Rennie had never heard her talk like this about their father before. "Where's Jarem now? Someone told me they might arrest him, too."

"I don't know where he is. He was furious when Poppa refused to help. He ran off and didn't want me to come with him. He'll probably never speak to me again."

"I'm sure it was just the heat of the moment."

"You didn't see him."

"Maybe you should go to his house."

"I think I need to give him time."

Rennie didn't want to push her. "All right. We need to make a plan for tomorrow, anyway. I'm really worried, Ayva. You can't let yourself be picked!"

"I don't even care anymore."

"You will care. Lifelong service to the immortals? I can't imagine anything worse, except maybe what happened to Belic. Getting picked for the defenders and then having to run away with Ares on your tail because things went so badly."

Ayva's face turned ashen at the mention of the immortal.

"I'll come with you if you want to run away tonight," Rennie said.

"Where would we go?"

"I don't know. South to the Savagelands?"

"The Savagelands? They say no one can survive there."

"Then we follow the trails north."

"We'll get lost."

"I've got a map. It only shows the main roads, but I also have a compass we can use to keep us in the right direction."

"It sounds much too risky. What about food and water along the way?"

"We can carry some."

"This isn't a plan. It's an act of desperation."

They heard the door opening in the front room. "Poppa," Ayva hissed. "Tell him I'm ill and can't make supper."

Rennie kissed the side of her head. "We'll talk more later."

To Rennie's surprise, Poppa's mood appeared normal, as if he had not been the slightest bit affected by the possibility of his daughter's boyfriend's family being sent to the gallows. He sniffed audibly and glanced around the kitchen. "What's for dinner?"

"Ayva's sick. We'll have to forage for something."

Only now did his expression darken. "Oh that child. She was almost as troublesome as you today." He opened the pantry, then shut it again and put his jacket back on. "I'll get dinner out." He left the house without offering to take the girls with him, or to bring anything back for them.

A glance in the pantry told Rennie that no one, not even Ayva, had made time to replenish its contents this week. She reached for a loaf of stale bread.

24

TOMMIS

The conversation with his mother continued to roll through Tommis's mind. He'd always loved her, despite that she'd allowed this brute of a man to become his father. Most likely, she hadn't a clue just how cruel and vindictive he could be when she married him. In those early days, he may have even been nice to her. It astonished Tommis sometimes, how deceptively charming his father could be around other people when he needed something from them.

Pa didn't attack Ma often, but when he did, Tommis couldn't bear to watch. Him, at over six feet and at least two hundred fifty pounds, and her, barely above five and just skin and bone. Talk about bullies. It was a wonder she was still alive.

The one time he'd tried to stop his father from punching her, Pa had switched his fury on him and broken his arm. Since then, Tommis had avoided interfering whenever Pa was taking out his anger on his mother. He hated himself for his cowardice, but vividly recalled the agony of the sharp bone sticking out of his skin, and couldn't bear facing anything similar again.

Ma was right, too. If she tried to leave, he would just kill her. Skalbourne had little oversight regarding who lived and who died, and by what means. If it was something with no bearing on the lives of the immortals, the authorities were not encouraged to investigate. Mortals could carry on however they liked, so long as they didn't inconvenience their masters. Tommis understood this. How mortals behaved toward one another could hold little interest for the immortals, with far loftier matters to concern them.

Tommis felt it deeply that the Rite would mark his transition into a man. As Aphrodite had said, only the weak allowed life to just happen to them. Once he was a man, he could not let his father dictate his actions anymore.

These were the thoughts that guided his decision. He had little time to prepare; it must be tonight. Through a single act, he could save Ma and him both. Himself to become a defender, and her to manage on her own, selling her flowers, her knitting, and her embroidery. Her living expenses would be near nothing without having to supply Pa with glutton-sized meal portions and gallons of liquor.

First thing in the morning, after his father went out to continue the roof repair, Tommis got out Pa's hidden stash of savings that he'd discovered long ago. Most likely Pa wouldn't have time to count it today. Yesterday, he had been so exhausted from a day's work, he'd fallen asleep instantly after stuffing down his food and drinking only two flagons of beer.

After taking some coins and restoring the remainder, Tommis went to Mrs. Robin's hideaway. Everybody knew she produced the strongest spirits around. Strictly speaking, selling it was forbidden, but the law rarely got enforced, possibly because the immortals understood enforcement would lower their popularity for no good reason.

Tommis told Mrs. Robin he was looking for a special gift. "The strongest whiskey you got. My father said you make the best."

She gave a self-satisfied smile and disappeared into the back room. A moment later, she returned with a small bottle filled with golden liquid. "This'll take the hair off his head."

"Can I get a larger one?"

"It'll cost you."

"I can afford it."

She returned with a bottle three times the size and he bought it.

Tommis spent the rest of his day catching rats and adding coins to the pile he already had. He returned home shortly before Pa. As expected, his father was in a foul mood following a day spent laboring. "Where's my dinner?" He sunk his bulk into his chair at the table, expecting instant service.

Tommis had told Ma in the morning how he was arranging a surprise for his father and hoped to cheer him up when he got home. She had volunteered to help by preparing Pa's favorite meal.

"Dinner's almost ready," she said. "I got your favorite cheese from farmer Chaison, and fresh bread from the baker. I'm cooking up cheese toasties for everyone."

Pa looked confused, like he still really wanted to be mad at everyone, but it was hard when Ma was being so nice. Tommis sat across from him. "I took your advice and made good money today." He poured out the coins he'd stolen earlier from Pa's stash, along with his actual earnings.

Pa's eyes widened. "See, that's what I mean. I knew you could do better."

Before Pa could ask more about it, Tommis handed him the bottle of whiskey. "I even had enough left over for this. Thought you might like it after working so hard the last couple days."

"Not sure you should be wasting our hard-earned money. The cheap stuff'll get you just as shitfaced." But Pa took out the stopper and his face brightened as he sniffed it. "Get me my glass, Ma."

He downed his first pour with a single gulp before refilling. It wasn't his habit to share with Ma, and tonight was no different. She was better off without it, thought Tommis.

"Oh, that warms the belly. Where are those cheese toasties?" Pa said.

Ma carried over a large plate of them, all melty and bubbly on top.

"Doesn't look like enough," Pa said.

"That's just for you. There's more coming for us." She returned with a generous plate for Tommis, and a small one for her. By then, Pa had already finished off two and replenished his glass again.

When the meal was over, Pa kept drinking while Tommis and Ma did the cleanup. Before long, he went out to take a leak, and when he stumbled back in, he went straight to the back room. Tommis heard him fall on the bed. The empty liquor bottle lay sideways on the table.

Tommis's body tingled in anticipation. Maybe it was fear, or more likely, hesitation over the terrible crime he was about to commit. And yet Aphrodite had practically suggested it. His father was a monster. Maybe that was justification enough.

"Ma, I forgot my best cap at Mrs. Robin's house. You mind going there and fetching it for me?"

She didn't seem bothered or surprised by the request.

"All right, just let me get my shawl." He hoped the errand would keep her busy for the next hour or two.

After she went out, he sat in Pa's armchair, screwing up his courage and waiting for the liquor to have its full effect. Before long, his father's ungodly snoring emerged from the room.

I have to act now. While Ma is away. While Pa's head is spinning. It has to be now.

But already he was having second thoughts. Must he kill him? Maybe Pa would be so content when he woke in the morning, he wouldn't oppose Tommis at the Rite. Or maybe the liquor would keep him sedated till it was over.

But Aphrodite would say this was leaving matters to chance. Pa could still prevent him from volunteering tomorrow. And if he didn't receive the mark either, he'd have hell to pay at home when Pa discovered the money missing from his cache. Probably the fiend would go right for the second earlobe. Tommis cringed to think what body part might be next once the lobes were gone.

A growling snore drew Tommis's attention again. It was now or never. He rose and took the thick pillow Pa used with his favorite chair. He'd chosen this method as least likely to arouse suspicion. Authorities might not check carefully into deaths, but if something obvious occurred, like a butcher knife sticking out of Pa's chest, they would be obliged to investigate. Suffocation, on the other hand, ought to look like his heart gave out.

Tommis squared his shoulders before entering the back room. Pa was sprawled face-up on the bed, still dressed in his work clothes. He must've passed out immediately. His mouth hung wide open, with spit drooling from both sides of it. Tommis took this perfect positioning as a sign it was meant to be.

He smashed the pillow over Pa's face, leapt on top of him, and pressed down with all his might.

But this was what it took to bring Pa to life. Full of fury, like a bear whose hibernation was cut short. Thrusting his torso, kicking his legs, grabbing with his huge, meaty hands. Pa was so much bigger and heavier than him. Tommis grappled to keep the pillow over his face without getting knocked off while Pa scratched and clawed at him.

With a sudden, monumental lunge, Pa flung Tommis and the pillow to the ground. He paused, coughing and sucking in air until he could speak again.

"You're trying to kill me?!" he roared. "You'll pay for this, you little shit!"

Before Tommis could crawl out of the way, Pa pounced on him and grasped him around the neck. Squeezing, squeezing. Tommis was the wild bucking horse now, the reverse of the situation just minutes ago. But Pa was the far stronger of the two, and Tommis grew weaker by the second with his breath cut off. *The fucker's going to kill me this time.*

Then, like a miracle, Pa let go. He grimaced in confusion and tried to stand up. Tommis slid sideways out from under him, right before Pa doubled over and vomited a bucket load of half-digested cheese.

The stench was almost enough to make Tommis throw up too. He clambered to the doorway and paused to look back.

With a beet-red face, Pa clutched his stomach in agony. The remains of his meal exploded out both ends now. Tommis turned away in disgust, rubbing his sore neck, until his father collapsed on the floor in a heap. Pa twitched for another minute before going still.

Ma walked into the room and stared down at her

husband without a shred of sympathy in her face. "I think that's done it then."

Tommis blinked at her.

"All the arsenic around here came in handy for once. His cheese toasties were full of it." She glanced around the room. "Let's clean up."

25

JAREM

After leaving Council Hall, Jarem rambled without direction through Gnarl Wood. He had never felt so useless before. He had been to the guardhouse, and he had pleaded their case to the highest official in Skalbourne. What more could he do? Petition an immortal? He was certain Apollo would not help them after the way his mother spoke to him the other day. How would he even contact any other immortal? Before Apollo, Moros had overseen Skalbourne, but he hadn't been seen for some time now.

Jarem also feared drawing attention to himself any further than he already had. What Ayva's father had said about his participation in the crime of concealing his brother's existence worried him. If the authorities arrested him, what hope would there be for any of them? As long as he maintained his freedom, he might still save them somehow. At the moment, he couldn't imagine how, but as long as they remained alive, he would never give up.

After he had crisscrossed the forest paths for hours, his stomach cried out for food. Jarem wasn't the type to lose his appetite in a crisis. Rather, he understood from a practical standpoint that action requires fuel, and only a fool would deliberately skip a meal.

He debated if he should go home, where they had a well-stocked pantry, or if he should buy something in town. The question was whether defenders might be waiting to arrest him outside his front door. In the end, he took the chance returning to his house. Better to know right away if they were after him, rather than slinking through town and jumping behind a lamppost every time a defender crossed the road, just in case.

With relief, he found everything as he'd left it. No one lurking around, and the doors locked. He got right to making a rabbit stew, at the same time snacking on a bowl of walnuts to stave off hunger until the meal was ready. While the meat and vegetables simmered in a pot, he sat down at the chessboard and played against himself the way Fenn did, trying to divert his thoughts from the suffering of his mother and brother at the guardhouse.

Unfortunately, both were losing sides in the game against himself and he grew bored. The stew still wasn't ready, and something seemed wrong about the way it smelled. It needed sage, he realized. There ought to be some in the garden. He went out and managed to find it without a lantern, though the sun was nearly set.

But just as he bent to pick the leaves, he heard approaching horses and froze at the sight of four defenders riding toward the house. Before he could react, one rider spotted him. "Over there!" she called to the others.

They're here to arrest me. If they succeeded, it would mean the end of his entire family. His only chance to save them all lay in escape. This thought propelled him toward the back of the property, across the clearing, into the woods.

Not on any trail, but into the most unruly section of close-grown trees, brush, and vines. He counted on the horses not being able to follow him into this terrain, at least not at anything above a walking pace. This only meant the defenders would dismount and chase him on foot. There were four of them, and all it took was one to be faster than him.

But he had been training daily for the Rite and was the fastest he would ever be in his life.

"That way!" another defender shouted.

Branches clawed at Jarem like they were in league with his pursuers. Scraping his skin and hooking his clothing, costing him precious seconds to extract himself. The forest cried out against his intrusion, with leaves crackling, branches snapping, and birds shrieking. The defenders might not be able to see him, but they could hear him.

He had an idea and changed his direction, only to have his foot catch on a root, sending him sprawling into the nearest tree. His head slammed against it and his vision blackened; he leaned on the wood, stunned.

"I see him!" the same defender called out.

Jarem's vision cleared, but the throbbing pulses inside his skull made him double in agony. When he placed his hand on his head, a huge welt rose beneath his fingers..

Run, he told himself. *I have to run.* Hadn't he been training for exactly this? The Trial would be no different. Fleeing stalkers, battling the unknown, forcing himself to keep going even when the pain was excruciating. If he failed in this, he wasn't worthy of the Trial.

He moved one foot ahead of the other, and again until he was sprinting, but not at his earlier pace. His pursuers sounded nearer than before. He forced his legs to move faster until, moments later, he broke out into the open. Now was when his lead would matter the most.

He'd arrived at the field of boulders where he and Mother had encountered Apollo the other day. Mounds of granite replaced the jumble of trees and overgrowth from which he emerged. He scrabbled to the top of one rock face, hesitating only a second before leaping across to another. He barely made it, with one knee banging against the stone. Compared to the pounding still going on in his head, it felt like nothing.

He climbed back down to ground level, out of their line of sight. He needed to use this time well. The place he was seeking shouldn't be much farther, if he could find it.

He recalled a bent pine struggling to maintain its hold on life marked the spot. A spark of hope filled him when it came into view. He lurched forward to the slab of rock backing it, that blended so well with another granite column behind it. In fact, there was a narrow gap between them, just wide enough for a man to slip through. He did so now, entering the cave that was larger than the inside of his house. At least, that was the way he remembered it. Now, with night almost fallen, he found himself plunged into total darkness.

Jarem felt his way along the rock wall until certain he was far enough from the entrance to be invisible to anyone who glanced in. He leaned against the cold stone and sucked in deep breaths that stank of mold and maybe even a rotting animal carcass. His head felt like someone was hammering it from the inside.

If they found him now, there would be no escape. They would slaughter him right here or capture him to return to the guardhouse. They had knives and swords; he was defenseless. His only chance lay in their missing the entrance to the cave, or not doing a thorough search inside it. He sank onto the ground, spread out on his back and prayed for sleep or even death to relieve his misery.

Time passed with no one approaching. He drifted in and out of sleep until a noise woke him. He thought it must be some kind of animal and strained his ears to the sound. It made the skin prickle on the back of his neck when he heard a groan that most definitely came from someone inside the cave.

He sprang to his feet and spun around. More groans followed, and they stretched on long enough for Jarem to tell that the man must be in a great deal of pain. His instinct told him he should flee the cave immediately, but compassion stayed him.

"Who are you?" he said.

The man fell silent. Jarem inched toward where the sounds had been coming from. His eyes were now partly accustomed to the darkness, allowing him to make out the outline of someone lying on the cave floor.

"B...B...Belic," the boy said.

"Belic? I'm Jarem. Aren't you a defender?" He had a moment of panic thinking this must be one of his pursuers. But then, how had he come to be wounded and alone inside this cave?

"...ran away from them... "

Jarem knelt beside him. "What happened to you?"

"...they stabbed me..."

"You need a doctor," Jarem said, without considering how he could fetch one, considering he was also a fugitive now.

"...take the med..." Belic trailed off, then tried again. "Take the medallion."

"What are you talking about?"

THE TRIALS

"Around my neck... important."

"Why should I take it?

"The immortals... don't want us to have it."

"We need to get you help first. I'll get someone from your family." The idea of saving Belic gave him fresh purpose. He stood up and made his way toward the opening, then an ominous feeling swept through him that the boy might die before he could return with help. "Belic?"

The boy didn't answer. Jarem hurried back to his side, to test if there might be any way he could carry him. In his own weakened state, he doubted it. "Belic?"

Still no response. Jarem bent lower, entreating Belic to speak to him and trying without success to catch the sound of his breathing. He touched the boy's frigid arm and then pressed his neck, searching for a pulse that wasn't there.

At the realization that Belic was dead, Jarem felt his own breath leave him. The cave was stifling, he needed to get out. He stumbled to the opening and gasped for air.

After a few moments of deep breathing, he wanted to leave, but he forced himself back into the cave to where Belic lay. As gentle as if Belic were still alive, he removed the medallion. Then he closed the boy's eyes. "Rest in peace, brother," he whispered.

Feeling his way back to the entrance, Jarem slipped out and scrambled across the boulders. He returned to the heavy cover of trees but lacked the energy to travel any farther. Curling under the canopy of an evergreen with low-hanging branches, he told himself that in the morning, he would find a way to inform Belic's family where they could find him. He would also decide what should be done with the medallion.

Soon after, he lost consciousness again.

26

TOMMIS

Tommis and Ma raced to clean up the mess in under an hour, knowing that Pa's body would soon stiffen and then questions would be asked about why they hadn't sent for the doctor sooner. Incredibly, they got Pa settled into his bed in such a way, it was almost possible to believe he died peacefully in his sleep. Then, on Ma's instruction, Tommis went out, woke their neighbor Paul, and paid him to fetch Dr. Hale.

When Tommis got back, Ma told him, "You leave this to me. You got nothing to do with it."

"But Ma…"

"Shush now. Wait for the doctor."

Before long, Tommis drifted into a restless slumber. It was still night, though, when Ma shook him back awake.

"He's here," she whispered.

Tommis knew what that meant. Time to put on the pretense of mourning.

Ma let the doctor in. "Thank you for coming," she said.

"I'm sorry for your loss," he said.

"A terrible loss it is, him with a son still at home."

Tommis made like he was wiping a tear. The doctor eyed him like he wasn't quite buying it. "I'll need to look at the body," he said.

"Follow me." Ma led him into the back room, where Pa appeared as they'd left him, except paler.

"How did it happen?" Dr. Hale asked.

"We went to bed early. He was snoring like usual, then he went all quiet. That's what woke me. I'm used to his noise, it's only when it stops I get worried. First I thought he went out to piss, but I reached over and felt him. He was still warm. I sat up and checked his breath after that. Nothing, he was gone."

Tommis watched the back of Dr. Hale from the doorway while the doctor verified Pa wasn't breathing and had no pulse, though it was easy to tell he was dead by just looking at him.

"Did he complain of any indigestion before bed?"

Tommis almost laughed; it was lucky Dr. Hale wasn't looking his way. Ma kept her face blank and shook her head.

"Did he mention anything else? A headache? Stomach pains? Fatigue?"

"Well now, he said nothing about that, but I know he was near dropping with exhaustion when he got home. He was out all day fixing a roof, and it was more work than he'd done in months."

The doctor pushed Pa's mouth open with difficulty since the rigor was setting in. He looked inside, sniffed, and furrowed his brow. Next, he unbuttoned Pa's pajama top and poked around his chest and stomach. He paused and turned around to look at Tommis.

"Did you see or hear your father get up during the night?" he asked.

"N—no, sir. I was tired." Tommis's nerves were making

him stutter. "I was s-so knocked out Ma had to shake me like a rag doll to wake me up."

The doctor's gaze hung on him for a moment longer, like he was waiting for a confession or something. Tommis clasped his hands to keep them from trembling and looked down at the floor. What if Dr. Hale figured out how Pa died, and what if he thought Tommis was the one to do it? Ma would protest, but he might think she was just protecting him. If he were arrested, he would never get to be a defender. Worse, the punishment for murder was hanging.

At last the doctor pulled the cover back up over Pa. "Let's go to the kitchen," he said.

He took out parchment from his bag and wrote Pa's name at the top. "The death certificate." He entered the time and date of Pa's passing. For cause, he wrote, "Heart failure," before adding his signature at the bottom. "You shouldn't have any trouble, Mrs. Spyke. The coroner will be here by morning to take the body away." He glanced from Ma to Tommis, reaching forward suddenly and touching his ear where the lobe was missing. "Sorry for your loss," he said again.

After the doctor went out, Ma turned to Tommis. "Remember when he sewed up your ear? He came a few times to treat my injuries too. Don't think he liked Pa much."

Ma had been very specific about which doctor Paul was to fetch. Now Tommis understood why. Ma was proving herself to be far more capable than he had ever imagined.

"Try to get some more sleep now," she told Tommis.

He got into his bed in the corner, while Ma settled on the comfortable chair that Pa forbade anyone from using except him, and pulled a blanket over herself. Tommis suspected she would never sleep in the marital bed again.

No sooner had he dozed off than he fell into a nightmare

involving Pa's ghost coming after him with a cleaver. He looked horrific in the afterlife, like he did before they cleaned him up. Thankfully, Tommis woke quickly, and despite his fear that Pa might prove even more formidable and terrifying in death than he was in life, he felt no remorse for his part in the killing. The satisfaction of seeing his father brought down was worth all manner of potential future suffering.

Another knock came at the door after dawn. Ma let in two large men, who wrapped Pa in a cloth and carried him away in a rickety cart. Her eyes shone as she shut the door forever on that miserable chapter of her life. *No remorse.*

Tommis's thoughts turned to the Rite, only hours away from starting. He wanted to look his best for what was going to be the most significant event of his life so far. After pouring scalding water into the tub, he used the soapy washcloth to scrub his scalp and body so hard it drew blood in a few places. But after working a long time on his fingers, he had to accept that the dirt under his nails had left a permanent stain.

He took pleasure in drying off with the one plush towel they owned, which Pa had reserved for himself only. He was about to go hunt in the back room for his nicer pants and shirt stored in the recess, when Ma handed him a neatly folded stack of clothing through the side of the privacy curtain.

"I saved up and got these for you," she said.

The new black trousers and crisp white linen shirt filled him with confidence once he put them on. When he came out, he found a shiny pair of leather shoes waiting for him as well. Ma must've measured his foot length one night while he was sleeping, because the fit was perfect.

Breakfast was ready on the table. Ma had rounded up

some eggs for them, along with fresh bread and honey. It tasted better than any meal he'd ever had.

He set out for the temple two hours before the ceremony was due to start. It was his plan to sit at the front and be the first to volunteer. That would show his enthusiasm to the immortals. If he waited till after someone else stepped forward, it might look as though he were influenced by that person instead of having made up his own mind well in advance.

"I'll come in time." His mother squeezed him around the waist. "So proud of you."

"Thanks for everything, Ma," he said. *No remorse.*

27

AYVA

During the night, Ayva remained awake in her room, listening for Poppa's return. She finally heard his footsteps entering the house close to midnight. The sounds moved into his bedroom, but she waited another quarter hour to be sure he was asleep, before rushing out of the house and not slowing down till she reached Jarem's. She couldn't bear the idea of his suffering alone, with nothing to think about but the tragic fate awaiting his family.

It surprised her to find his front door ajar. She poked her head into the house. "Hello? Jarem?"

Silence greeted her, along with the scent of rabbit stew. The pot sat on the stove with the flame gone out.

She continued through the rest of the place, past a cozy living area, into what must have been his mother's bedroom, and then into a room with two beds for the boys. She admired a cane she found lying on one of the bedspreads. It had to be Jarem's handiwork, because he was skilled in woodworking and had made her a beautiful jewelry box for her last birthday. How thoughtful to fashion something so useful for his brother, she thought.

But where was he? The time was nearly one in the morning. Could he have gotten good news that his mother and brother were being released, and he needed to come fetch them? That would explain the haste that caused him to leave the door ajar.

But the chill she felt inside her was saying something different. What if defenders had arrested him too? Her father had said he was just as culpable as his brother. She wouldn't even put it past Poppa to have issued the warrant.

Nothing looked out of order inside the house, though. Wouldn't there have been a struggle? She couldn't imagine Jarem allowing them to take him without a fight, but the only sign of anything amiss had been the open door.

What were her options? Go back home, wake her father, and demand to know if Jarem was arrested? But Poppa had already made it clear he would not allow her to influence him. She could not help Jarem that way.

But if he had gone out for some other reason, and if there was any chance of his coming back tonight, she could comfort him and make him feel less alone. At the very least, she needed to wait a few hours before giving up on his return. She curled up with a blanket on the wide armchair in the living room, and despite her concerns, she drifted to sleep.

She was woken in the morning by Rennie shaking her. "Ayva, it's me."

Ayva looked around. "I slept too long. Has Jarem come back?" She squinted at the sharp slab of sunlight cutting across the floor from the window.

"No one's here. Where is he?"

"I don't know. He hasn't been here all night. I was waiting, hoping he'd come home. Did Poppa tell you anything? Was Jarem arrested?"

"Poppa didn't say. This morning he was furious when he discovered you were gone. I told him I'd find you and get you to the Rite on time."

"Is it that late?"

"We have to be quick."

A feeling of listlessness came over Ayva. "If only I knew what happened to him."

"Don't think about that now. We need to get you ready. Come here."

She led Ayva to the table and took scissors out of her bag.

"My hair?" Ayva frowned and clutched a lock of it.

"I think you should let me cut it like a boy's."

If Jarem was arrested, she didn't care what happened to her. But she would cooperate with the plan for her sister's sake. Rennie snipped furiously to deliver a short, choppy cut that looked like a three-year-old did the job. Ayva gave a short laugh when she looked in the mirror, but she didn't care.

"We should dress you like a boy, too." After a brief search of the brothers' bedroom, Rennie found worn clothes from when they were younger and smaller. Still, the pants required a belt to keep them from falling down on Ayva.

Rennie stepped back to appraise her. "Still beautiful, but not so elegant. You should keep your face lowered. Don't look anyone in the eye. And slump your shoulders like this." Rennie demonstrated.

When Ayva looked down, she noticed the gold band on the fourth finger of her right hand, and had a sudden realization. She pulled off the ring and held it out to Rennie. "Take this."

Her sister looked at her in horror. "What? No. You keep it."

"They'll take it from me if I'm chosen."

"That will be an added incentive to try to avoid that fate."

"It's not under my control. Please, Rennie. Momma would want one of us to have her wedding ring. Poppa would too."

Rennie hesitated, not so certain regarding Poppa's feelings on the matter.

"If I'm not chosen, you can give it back to me. All right? There's some incentive."

Rennie didn't object as Ayva pushed the ring onto her finger and squeezed her hand. "I want to go now," Ayva said.

28

AYVA

They were among the last to arrive at the temple. Ayva scanned the room looking for Jarem, but the sixteens always sat in the front pews, and there was no chance of glimpsing them from the back of the dark and voluminous hall. Especially since the families and friends of every participant filled the remaining seats, overflowing into the aisles in some sections.

"Name?" an official asked.

"Ayva Tallis." She looked down at the table where only two birth records remained: hers and Jarem's. Wouldn't they have removed his document if he'd been arrested? She wondered now if he had fled Skalbourne. It broke her heart to think he might have gone without her, though she understood if it had been the only way to avoid arrest.

"Take your seat," the official said.

Rennie grasped her elbow and guided her along the center aisle. She could not have done it without her sister's help. Hissing voices echoed in all directions, and angry gazes bore into them. Clearly she and Jarem were being blamed for holding up the proceedings.

"Hurry up!" screeched Mrs. Grindle, the baker's wife, whose son Wolder was among the sixteen. Ayva glanced up at the woman's face twisted in fury. Strange, she had never had a cross word for Ayva before. The Rite changed people; made them selfish and protective of their own. By contrast, the giant stained glass window facing them depicted Zeus addressing a sheepish group of mortals with heads bent in submission.

Rennie led her to the first pew occupied by the sixteens, who squeezed closer to make room for her. Her sister kissed the side of her head and whispered, "Whatever happens, I love you forever and ever." Rennie stepped backward and knelt next to the pew behind her.

Ayva noticed Poppa glaring in her direction from where he sat at the head of the council. She'd seen his anger directed at Rennie before, but never at her. He would not forgive either of them if she wasn't chosen as a blest. Rennie would be blamed for cutting her hair, and she for consenting to it. But Ayva no longer cared what he thought. Even if it meant she and her sister would have to move away, earn their own keep, and never see their father again.

She had no concern for anyone but Jarem. In response to every sound that seemed to come from near the entrance, she turned her head to see if it was him. The depth of her despair deepened each time he failed to appear.

Before long, trumpets announced the arrival of the attending immortal. Not Moros, who had been in charge for years, but Apollo, who had taken over at the most recent Welcoming. He had a far more regal appearance than his predecessor, striding down the aisle with his face beaming, as if this were actually a joyful occasion instead of a miserable duty that could end in the death of several of those chosen.

THE TRIALS

And still no Jarem.

Apollo took his place in front to address both the sixteens and the general assembly. "Greetings," he began. "Today we welcome all who have celebrated their sixteenth birthday in the past year. As of today, you have officially come of age, and now possess all the rights and responsibilities due to adults.

"As part of these new responsibilities, twelve among you will be selected to take part in the Trials. Those who successfully complete them shall be named Defenders of the Realm. It is a high honor to become a defender, a position of tremendous responsibility that places you closer to the immortals. Only the most accomplished mortals, possessing the greatest amount of integrity, receive this opportunity. The rewards are vast, both in this life and the next, for those who perform their service to the highest standards.

"As part of our tradition, we allow the sixteens the opportunity to volunteer for the Trials before the remainder of the competitors are chosen at random. This is because enthusiasm and dedication are among the qualities—"

Sounds of a commotion drew everyone's eyes toward the hall entrance. Ayva rose to see the door flung open, and Jarem backing into the temple. Metal clashed furiously as he struggled to hold off three defenders with the parries of his sword. An uproar occurred as people in the aisles hastened to shift out of the way.

Jarem was on fire, dancing between his attackers with his sword swishing wildly, blocking one and then another of his opponents' thrusts. But three were too many. The middle one lunged and knocked the sword from his hand. The others leapt forward, grasped his arms, and pinned them behind his back. Ayva screamed as the middle one prepared to strike again.

"Stop!" Apollo's voice rang out.

The defenders looked confused, but unquestioning obedience to the immortals took precedence over any other consideration. The swordsman lowered his weapon.

Now that Jarem was still, Ayva could see the sorry state he was in. A massive lump on his head, bruises on his arms and legs, nicks and cuts all over his body. It was a wonder he'd made it there alive.

Before the immortal could continue, Jarem shouted, "My name is Jarem Woodgard and I offer myself to the Trials!"

A shocked silence fell over the temple. Jarem's turning up should've filled Ayva's heart with joy. But instead she felt it dissolve into ash on hearing his words: *I offer myself to the Trials*. She clutched her arms around her waist, rocking back and forth in agony, knowing that whatever the outcome here today, he was lost to her.

"Release him," Apollo said. "Allow him to come forward."

29

TOMMIS

Tommis had been waiting to volunteer as soon as Apollo finished his speech, when that son of a bitch Jarem interrupted everything and beat him to it. He should've been skewered on the spot, or at the very least arrested and dragged away for the crime of harboring a defective. Instead, the immortal allowed him to come ahead of others who obeyed the law and arrived on time. It was just like Jarem to steal everyone else's thunder and get away with it.

He tried to quell his furious thoughts. *The immortals know best. The immortals know best.* He forced himself to focus on this truth while Jarem approached Apollo, kneeled before him with his head bowed, and repeated his words from a moment earlier: "My name is Jarem Woodgard. I offer myself to the Trials."

"The immortals accept your offer," Apollo said. "Wait now in the place of honor."

Jarem rose and moved to the section decorated with garlands that was reserved for the twelve who would be selected. Tommis tasted venom at the back of his throat.

Apollo addressed the sixteens again. "Any others who would like to volunteer, please step forward now."

Tommis sprang to his feet to be certain he didn't get supplanted again. But he was the only one, making him feel ridiculous about being in such a hurry to beat out nobody. Several people in the assembly snickered.

"Come forward," Apollo told him.

As he moved to the aisle, someone stuck out their foot and tripped him. He landed flat on the floor, humiliated, with the muffled laughter of other sixteens echoing inside his head. His gaze shifted to Ayva, who was turned away. Another sign that she no longer cared what happened to him. Not a thought for anyone but *fucking Jarem*.

He scrambled to his feet and a moment later spoke the words that would seal his fate: "I am Tommis Spyke. I offer myself to the Trials." He was told to wait with Jarem.

There were no more volunteers. Apollo thanked Tommis and Jarem "For their enthusiasm and devotion to the immortals." Polite clapping followed. Tommis spotted Ma in the assembly with her face glowing.

"The remaining ten will be chosen now." Apollo nodded toward several officials who were to distribute the folded slips of parchment that were either blank or bore the large black *X* indicating selection. "Wait until I give the command to open them."

A hushed silence fell over the assembly while squares were handed out. Tension hung in the air as the moment approached that would transform the lives of some of them forever.

"You may open your parchment now."

There was a collective second or two of hesitation before the opening began. A boy cried out on seeing the mark; a girl screamed. No one wanted to receive it, of course. If they'd wanted the job, they would've volunteered.

Tommis followed Jarem's gaze to Ayva, who gave him a subtle shake of her head. *Not chosen.*

One by one, those selected were called forward to declare their names and offer themselves to the Trials. The girl who had screamed continued to wail and had to be carried to the front. When she sobbed out the words that were expected of her, Tommis almost felt sorry for the frail little thing. He couldn't imagine her as a defender, but maybe that was her own fault for not preparing herself physically, as all children were expected to do.

"Let us thank these initiates and wish them success in the Trials," Apollo said.

The applause was louder than before, though some in the assembly wept. No doubt the parents and siblings of those who were chosen.

Tommis and the remaining twelve were escorted from the hall.

30

RENNIE

It felt like a nightmare from which Rennie couldn't awake when Jarem slammed into the building battling three swordsmen. Of all the Rites she had attended, she'd never witnessed anything as wild as this.

The good news and the bad news were the same. Apollo had accepted Jarem's offer, meaning the boy was now obliged to undergo the Trials and, if successful, to become a defender. This had saved him from arrest and a possible hanging, but Ayva would be inconsolable over their separation.

That Tommis Spyke volunteered came as a shock too. She didn't know him well. He seemed aloof, like he didn't care to have any friends or to be part of the community. Yet he'd done a service for her sister some years ago and Ayva had long defended him from the cruel judgment of their peers. It appeared he preferred risking death in the Trials to spending his life catching rats like his father.

In the streets on the way to the assembly hall, she had overheard a woman telling someone else that Tommis's father's heart had given out last night. Grief made people do crazy things sometimes, and maybe this death was the catalyst that led him to volunteer. If so, it was unlucky for him to suffer such a loss the night before the Rite.

It was difficult to watch the misery of those selected by lottery. Mara moaned the loudest, but Rennie sympathized less with her because of how haughtily she behaved around others less fortunate than herself. Her mother was on the council, and Mara had been convinced she had the power to keep her from being picked. That would explain why she became hysterical when it happened.

If Rennie were to get chosen for something next year, she would rather it be the Trials than becoming a blest. At least as a defender, she would be trained to fight. A blest was only a glorified maidservant plus suspected other duties Rennie didn't want to think about. No one was so much at the mercy of the immortals as they.

Her gaze shot back to her sister. She wore the glazed look of someone who wasn't fully comprehending everything happening around her. It was all moving too fast, from the arrest of Jarem's mother and brother, to his disappearance last night, to his volunteering for the Trials to escape arrest. Rennie admired him for his quick thinking; otherwise, he'd be at the guardhouse right now, most likely awaiting a hanging with the rest of his family. But Ayva wasn't seeing it that way. Rennie knew her. She was thinking that her life was over, so what did it matter what happened next?

Rennie tried to channel her thoughts to her sister. *Wake up! Remember what I told you. Head down, shoulders slumped.* But Ayva wasn't listening. She sat straight up, staring forward with glistening eyes. If anything, she looked even more special than usual. There was an other-worldliness to her now that set her apart from the rest of the group. Her haircut was irrelevant. Her beauty came from the irrepressible quality of goodness inside her.

Apollo began. "Now we come to the choosing of the blest. Those who are picked receive the highest honor the immortals can bestow upon mortals. The blest live among us in Olympus, and those who serve with extreme dedication and devotion may attain immortality themselves. I will now walk among you and make this year's selections."

He started from the back, moving behind the remaining sixteens while they were obliged to keep their gaze straight ahead. First, he laid his hand upon a boy's shoulder. "You are blest. Go to the place of honor." The boy staggered toward the area recently vacated by the future defenders.

He did not look thrilled by the honor. They never did. Some merely trembled, like this one. Some passed out and had to be revived. In the worst case Rennie could recall, a boy had died upon feeling the immortal's hand on his shoulder.

Rennie had seen this boy before, though she couldn't remember his name. He was handsome, with delicate features and a shy demeanor. The typical pick for a blest.

Apollo had not passed Ayva's seat yet. But Rennie allowed herself to feel a little hope after Apollo selected a different girl as his next choice. Sometimes they only picked two. One of each gender; wasn't that enough for one year? But now and then, they picked more. Two years ago, there had been five.

This girl wasn't as beautiful as Ayva, but her manner was more submissive. And she was a different type. Wavy blond hair and pale white skin. Maybe this was what the immortals were favoring this year, and then Ayva would be safe.

Rennie held her breath as Apollo approached her sister. *Don't pause, don't pause. Keep going, keep going.*

As the immortal reached out to touch Ayva, Rennie slapped her hand over her mouth to keep from crying out. Her sister, to her credit, remained composed. Though her eyes shone like they were full of tears, she glided from her seat to the center of the room.

Apollo passed the rest of the row before returning to his place at the front of the assembly. "These three have been chosen. Let us congratulate them."

Rennie refused to take part in the applause. However, Poppa more than made up for her silence by clapping twice as hard as anyone else. It was a struggle not to despise him.

As the newly blest were led away, her sister glanced back and threw a kiss at Rennie. The realization that this would be the last time she ever saw Ayva fed the sprawling mass of resentment growing inside her. Rennie knew it was only a matter of time until it exploded out of her. She couldn't imagine what the consequences might be for herself or for everyone who stood in her way.

31

FENN

Based on the assumption that the guard brought him a meal at regular intervals three times a day, Fenn guessed this was the fourth morning since he and Mother had been arrested. He had asked for the date several times, but the guard never replied to any of his questions.

He couldn't hear other prisoners. He thought Mother must be in another section of the jail, maybe an area reserved for women. The door of his cell felt like solid metal except for what was probably a small window at face height for an average person. But even when the guard came in to deliver his meal, Fenn never caught a sound from anyone else. The sense of isolation weighed on his soul. He'd never felt like this at home, even though it had been a prison of another sort. The near constant presence of Jarem or Mother had prevented him from feeling utterly alone.

He missed fresh air nearly as much as companionship. The dank cell reeked of mold, shit, and dead animals. Plus other odors he couldn't identify. Breathing became a torture with his heightened sense of smell.

When they'd brought him here, they had shoved him into the room and banged the door shut. He'd had to feel his way along the perimeter to get a sense of its dimensions and contents. It was so cramped, the process didn't take long. His exploration of the walls turned up no windows, or at least not any within his reach. But he had found a thin, almost useless pad on the floor for sleeping, and a bucket in the corner for relieving himself. This was the source of much of the stench, since the guard emptied it infrequently.

Later, with nothing else to do, Fenn had calculated the area. His feet were approximately eleven inches long, a fact he knew from Mother measuring them every few months as he was growing up. Walking toe-to-heel alongside the wall, he counted six and a half steps, putting that side at six feet. In the other direction, he counted ten steps with his toe scrunched up at the end. Nine feet. Fifty-four square feet of living space. Maybe it would've been better not to know.

Most of the time, he sat on the pad, leaning against the wall, playing chess in his head. Fortunately, he didn't need to feel the board to envision the layout and movement of the pieces. He thought about his brother while he analyzed the game in the background of his mind. If he was correct in his counting of the days, the Rite was happening today. Knowing how much Jarem loved Ayva, he prayed hard that neither would be picked. Let them both be free of any service to the immortals, he thought. Let them marry, live happily, and bear children of their own. With luck, none would be blind.

As for himself, he was waiting for death. If the immortals didn't think his life worthy when he was born, they were not likely to have changed that opinion.

The fault for their arrest lay with him. He was the one who'd insisted on meeting Ayva, and since the arrest had occurred the very next day, his logical chess-playing brain told him the events had to be connected. Apollo must've been alerted by whoever learned the secret from Ayva—maybe her sister or father. The immortal had pretended to be interested in Mother's hunting skills as a pretext for looking around inside the house. Apollo had needed no proof beyond a chess board designed for the blind before sending in the troops.

Mother would almost certainly die because of his selfishness. He wished his own death would come sooner. He feared someone might inform him his mother had been executed. Having confirmation of his worst imaginings would only increase his torment. At least now he could still pray she might somehow escape.

After what he thought was the second meal of the day, he dozed. The clang of the cell door opening woke him.

"Get up." This was the first time the guard had spoken to Fenn.

"What for?" he asked.

"You're coming with me."

"Why?"

The guard kicked him. "Don't ask questions."

Fenn pulled himself up. This was it, then. The man was taking him to the gallows. Now that it was time, regret washed over him. He wished he could learn what had happened to Jarem at the Rite. And with the end nearly upon him, he clung to what had made life dear to him, despite its many deprivations. *The love of mother and brother.* A sudden wish to hear their voices once more before he died overwhelmed him.

The guard wrenched his arm and yanked him out of the cell. They trod through several corridors, Fenn listening as the guard paused with keys jangling, unlocking doors before they could proceed. At the fourth opening, the man pushed him through, causing him to trip on a step. He landed hard on his hands and knees.

The breeze on his cheeks told him he was outside. The air smelled fresh compared to what he just came from. He thought the guard would grasp him again and draw him back onto his feet, but he said, "You're free to go."

"What?" Fenn thought he must've heard wrong.

"You're free to go!"

"I am? What about my mother?"

"Not her. She'll hang at dawn."

"Let her go instead of me!"

The guard's footsteps echoed inside the building. The door slammed shut. Fenn shouted until his throat was hoarse, but no one opened the door again.

32

JAREM

Jarem and the other initiates were ushered out of the hall and into several wagons for transport to the defender outpost. They sat on hay bales that provided no cushion against the harsh movement of the carts. The incessant banging along the uneven road increased the throbbing inside his head. He looked down, speaking to no one and biting his lower lip to keep from moaning. Aching bruises and open wounds covered much of his body, and his hollow stomach cried out for a meal. He had no clue how he might complete a single trial.

He had escaped arrest, though. That had been his goal. After waking beneath the tree this morning, he had considered his options. He could flee Skalbourne with no help or preparation and pray the defenders didn't catch him. This was inconceivable; defenders brought in from other towns always helped line the borders on the day of the Rite.

There would be no hope for his family if every one of them languished in the guardhouse. But if instead he volunteered for the Trials, and if the immortals accepted his offer, and if he survived... it still might be too late to save them from the gallows. But it would not be too late for him to train as a defender, and someday, he didn't know when or how, to use those warrior skills to bring about change. He would crusade for justice in their names.

This was what he told himself. If he were to be completely honest, he would have to admit he craved life, and had long held a burning desire to become a leader among mortals. He'd always believed he was born to a higher calling than that of a simple carpenter, which was the path his mother and Ayva had expected him to follow.

His mind made up, he had returned home after making two necessary stops, and retrieved a sword from the stash of them his mother had hidden in the house for their defense. From there he'd gone directly to the Rite. When guards tried to block his entrance, he succeeded in battling past them into the hall, which was all he needed in order to catch Apollo's attention.

Only now that there were no more decisions to be made, he had time to think about Ayva. Was she a blest now? He hoped not, with all his heart, but he couldn't imagine her escaping the immortals' notice.

As they rounded the bend, he raised his head and squinted forward. The forest parted and a massive concrete fortress revealed itself. Age and foul weather had long darkened its surrounding walls, topped by sharp points of steel. Thick, black smoke billowed from its chimneys.

The wagons passed through its gates and wheeled up to what may once have been a grand entrance before its marble dulled and cracked. The twelve were ushered out of their conveyances into the building, along a dim hallway to a cavernous room with cots set out along two opposing sides.

Still no one spoke. After standing for a moment, Jarem's

head spun, forcing him to seek the nearest bed. His vision cleared after he sat down, and he took the time to glance at the others. He recognized everyone, though he did not consider them to be friends. In fact, there didn't appear to be strong connections among any of the group. Jarem watched as several others chose a bed and lay down with their faces pressed against their pillows.

One by one, they were taken out by guards and allowed to clean up. When it was Jarem's turn, he made cautious movements so as not to awaken the pounding in his head again, but a tall guard with white-blond hair and an evil smirk shoved him forward, banging his heavily bruised arm against the wall. He clenched his teeth and stepped up his pace. In the bathing room, the guards left him alone with a plentiful supply of soap and cold water. There was no hot water, nor any way to heat it, but compared to his other discomforts, it made little difference. He scrubbed himself vigorously, avoiding the painful lump on his head. Afterward, he changed into a uniform, green for initiates instead of the regulation dark blue that defenders wore.

"Do you know who they picked to be blest this year?" he asked the orderly who brought him the clothes.

The boy said, "I don't know their names. There are three of them, a boy and two girls. One of the girls, she's beautiful but odd-looking. I thought she was a boy at first, because of her clothes and how short her hair was cut. Maybe her family's poor."

Ayva. Jarem's heart sank. He'd seen her seated with the others, and understood right away that she was doing her best to avoid being picked. Recognizing her shirt as one that Fenn used to wear, he realized she must have come to his house last night. If only he could've been there to wrap her in his arms one last time.

Her effort had been wasted, though. She could've covered her face in mud and her bright light would still have shined through.

"They're here," the boy whispered. "Blest are housed on the second floor until they can be brought to their training."

Jarem's heart surged. "Will they join us for meals?"

"No. You aren't allowed to mingle."

Jarem was accompanied back to the dormitory, where he rested until all the initiates.had cleaned and changed into their new uniforms. Then the guards brought them to a vast dining hall, where rows of heavy oak tables and benches could have provided seating for far more than their small group. Giant tapestries depicting heroic deeds of the immortals lined the walls.

The scent of roasted game made Jarem delirious with hunger, but unfortunately, the meal didn't appear as soon as they settled at a table. The hysterical girl, Mara, sat on his left, while Kailo, a formidable boy whose shape resembled that of a bull standing on its rear legs, was on his right. Tommis, the disagreeable rat-catcher, scowled at him from across the table. A girl named Sareena smiled and rubbed her hands as she took a seat beside Tommis, and Brax, a thin, nervous fellow, slipped into the last empty spot.

Sareena was just opening her mouth to say something when the arrival of Captain Broyland was announced. He looked young for a captain, maybe in his mid-twenties, but he had a straight spine, raised shoulders, and a confident tone.

"Welcome, Initiates," he began. "I trust you're well-rested. And well-prepared, because we don't waste any time around here. Allow me to explain how this works.

"The course consists of three major trials, each more challenging than the one before it. Only one person runs the course at a time. In other words, one person will undergo the Trials each day for twelve days. There's a certain advantage to being the first, because waiting takes a mental toll, especially when news of deaths creeps in. And those who wait have no other diversion; it wouldn't be fair for us to allow them additional training.

"Therefore, we assign your place in the Trials at random. My assistant will distribute a folded paper to each of you. At my command, you will open them. A number from one to twelve will be written on it."

The air was tense as papers were handed out and everyone waited for permission to open them. When the captain gave the go-ahead, Jarem unfolded his with trembling fingers. *Number two.* For several seconds, he struggled for breath. Going second might be an advantage for some. But Jarem had wished for a few days to allow his wounds to heal, his head to stop pounding, his body to catch up on sleep, and his stomach to fill up with the food it needed.

The assistant made a note of the order of contestants, which the captain then read aloud. Of those at their table, Kailo was first, Jarem second, Sareena fifth, Tommis seventh, Brax eighth, and Mara eleventh.

It occurred to Jarem that the anxiety of waiting would destroy someone like Mara, and therefore she might be willing to switch places with him. "Sir," he waved his hand. "Is it possible for two people to switch if they both agree?"

"No." The captain was curt. "To those thinking that if they compete later in the challenge, they will benefit by learning about it from those who already took it, you can forget about that. You'll gain only one piece of information by day's end, and that is whether the contestant succeeded or not. Those who succeed don't return here, but are escorted to Olympus, where training to become a defender begins."

Jarem would not give it high marks for an inspiring speech, though he supposed it was accurate. The possibility of having to do the Trials provided motivation for a generation of children to maintain good physical and mental conditioning. From day one in Skalbourne, the strong and intelligent were favored, and the weak eliminated. This was just one more example of the way of life imposed on mortals by the immortals.

"I wish you all success," Captain Broyland concluded.

Sareena raised her hand, but the captain ignored her and left the room. Servers began delivering food to the tables, to Jarem's great relief.

"I was going to ask if we're allowed to carry weapons," Sareena said.

"I guess we'll be allowed to carry whatever they give us before we start," Jarem said.

"It's difficult to plan our strategy without knowing what we're dealing with."

A plate piled with sliced venison, roast potatoes, and green vegetables landed in front of Jarem. He wolfed down several bites of the meat before forcing himself to slow down to give his stomach time to settle.

"I don't know what you mean, *plan our strategy*. There's no strategy. We don't know what we're facing," Tommis said.

Mara's hand shook so hard holding her fork, it clattered against her plate. "We're all going to die," she muttered.

"The immortals won't let that happen," Tommis said. "How would they get new defenders?"

"I imagine it's very entertaining for them to watch us," Mara said.

"That's offensive." Tommis glanced around. "You better hope they're not listening."

"Oh lighten up," Sareena said, chewing with her mouth open. "Would someone pass the damn salt?"

33

FENN

Fenn needed to put aside thoughts about Mother and Jarem for now. His immediate problem was how to get back home. Feeling the rail beside him, he drew himself up. It sounded as if the road was nearby. He could hear wagons creaking, the clomp of horses' hooves, and footsteps on gravel. People passed close to him, talking, laughing, and calling out to one another.

He'd never been in town before. Jarem often spoke of having to dodge horse riders and carriages at busy times of the day. That could be right now, for all he knew.

He was pretty certain today was the Rite. From all the noises, it didn't seem like this was keeping people off the roads. Maybe the ceremony had ended and the temple had emptied out. Fenn didn't know the city's geography because he'd never needed to learn it. He could not have imagined a day when he would be wandering the streets by himself.

He would need to solicit the help of a kind stranger. Finding his home would be an impossible task otherwise. But no one seemed to notice him. He could understand why passersby might avoid the guardhouse. Still, it meant he'd have to take the initiative by walking toward the sounds. The idea of the horses frightened him the most. He thought they were towering creatures, but since they had never owned one, he had only a rough idea of their actual dimensions.

He took a cautious step and then another. So far, flat ground. He held out his hands to check for obstructions in front of him, praying he was not making a spectacle of himself.

Someone whistled and called out, "Hey, defective!" A chorus of voices shouting other phrases followed. "Blind boy," "Must be the Woodgard kid," and "Look at his eyes!" were some that he heard. Footsteps approached, along with the voices.

"Do you know my brother Jarem?" Fenn asked. If he could just find a friend of his brother's, that person would surely help him.

"He can talk," a man said.

"Of course I can talk." He couldn't believe the ignorance of people, thinking a blind man wouldn't be able to speak. "Could someone find me a stick? It will help me walk," Fenn said.

Someone made barking noises. "Doggie wants a stick, ruff, ruff."

Another man said, "I'll get you one."

A moment passed while Fenn congratulated himself on finding one helpful person. Then a sharp blow struck him at the back of his head, knocking him to the ground. Something clattered on the road beside him.

"There's your fucking stick," the man said.

The back of his head felt damp. *Bleeding*. These people were cruel. No one spoke out against whoever had dealt the blow. He patted the ground until he found the stick, and stood up. Using it to feel in front of him, he began walking away. Or what he thought might be *away*.

"Defective!" a woman shouted.

Quickening his pace, he stepped off an unexpected curb and fell again, twisting one of his ankles.

"Get out of our town, defective!"

Fenn heard running footsteps accompanied by younger voices. A group of children must've seen him and come over.

"His eyes are all white!" a girl screeched.

"Don't look at them!" a boy shouted. "He's like Medusa. If you look at his eyes, you'll turn to stone."

"Cover them!" another girl cried.

Before Fenn could rise, a large man jumped on his back and pulled a hood over his head. *They're going to smother me.* Fenn rolled over and kicked at him, but then a second person came. One held him while the other tied the cloth round his neck, choking him.

"We covered his eyes!" the man pinning him down called out. He released Fenn and backed away.

"He can't see, he can't be!" A group of young voices arose and made a chant of it. "Spin him around, make him frown. Knock him down, run him out of town."

Hands grabbed his arms and clothing, spun him roughly around, and let go. He lost his balance and fell hard against the side of a building, banging his forehead.

"Leave him alone!" a powerful voice rang out. "You should be ashamed of yourselves!"

To his surprise, Fenn heard the crowd dispersing.

Someone approached and touched his shoulder. "Are you all right?"

"My head hurts. I'm okay."

"Allow me to take this thing off you." The man or

woman, Fenn wasn't sure which, removed the hood. "I'm the loremaster," the person said. "What's your name?"

"Fenn."

"Would you like to take my arm, Fenn?"

"Thank you." In reaching for the arm, he discovered the person was quite small. He wondered how they commanded so much respect.

"I apologize for those ruffians. They rarely see anyone with different abilities than their own. It frightens them."

"I think I was far more frightened than they were. I thought they'd kill me."

"I don't think it would've gone that far. Shall I take you home?"

"Do you know where that is?"

"I do. I know your mother and brother. I would say Charlet is even a friend of mine."

"Is there any chance of saving her? They told me she'll be hung at dawn."

The loremaster grew silent for a moment. "I wish I could give you hopeful news. But many have lost babies to the law governing defectives, if I may use that repulsive word. The immortals wouldn't wish to deal with the amount of suppressed fury and resentment that would likely arise if any one individual escaped punishment for doing the thing everyone else wished they could have done—save their condemned infant."

He took a heavy breath. "I sincerely wish I could save Charlet. But I have no influence with the council. Nor with any of the immortals."

The answer was what Fenn had expected, and yet it sunk his heart to hear it from the loremaster, who sounded so authoritative and reasonable compared to the others. He moved on to the next subject of concern. "Was today the Rite? Do you know what happened to my brother?"

"I have better news to share with you here. Your brother volunteered for the Trials. This allowed him to avoid arrest."

Hope surged inside Fenn. Who would succeed at the Trials, if not Jarem? He had every confidence in his brother. But one thing confused him. "Why arrest him and let *me* go?"

"I'm not certain. But I've heard whisperings. Apollo may have said, *being blind is suffering enough*. Your experience today tends to bear that out."

"Maybe given time, they would've released Jarem too. Now I wish he hadn't volunteered," Fenn said.

"But he did. We must send prayers for his success."

"Do you know what happened to Ayva Tallis today?"

The loremaster sighed. "She will become a blest.

Fenn's chest tightened. He felt a kinship to Ayva, the girl who loved his brother and kindly offered to be his friend. He hoped she would flourish in her life as a blest.

Before the loremaster announced their arrival, Fenn knew they'd reached his home. How could he not recognize the smells surrounding it, the particular feel of the ground under his feet, and the sound of the wind blowing through the branches of their very own trees?

"Will you be all right if I leave you?" the loremaster asked.

"Yes, I can manage here without help."

"All right then. But I'll check on you from time to time, if you'll allow me. I can arrange for food and other necessities to be brought to you."

"Thank you, sir. You're very kind."

With that, the loremaster went on his way.

Fenn could do the rest. He knew his home. He climbed

up the steps, entered the house, and went straight to the room he shared with his brother. Used to share. Exhaustion drew him to his bed, where he started to lie down, but paused when he felt something hard beneath him. He picked up a walking stick, feeling the smoothness of its surface and the curve of its handle. He sniffed the wood, which still carried the scent of charred bark.

That Jarem had made a cane for him showed he'd clung to the belief that his brother would return home. Fenn vowed to do the same for him.

34

JAREM

After dinner, the dozen initiates were ordered to return to the dormitory. A few sat together on a corner bed and spoke in hushed voices among themselves. Jarem chose a place on the opposite side. His body, with all the healing it needed to do, cried out for sleep. It came as soon as he closed his eyes.

As he'd hoped by going to bed so early, he woke in the middle of the night. Only the heavy breathing of some of the sleepers broke the silence. For a moment, he lay staring through the nearest window at the starlit sky. There was no moon, which would likely be better for his purpose.

He sat up and glanced around. Everyone had gone to bed, but he imagined more than a few lay awake. Who could sleep for long with the threat of the Trials looming over them? He would have to take the chance that anyone who saw him would ignore him and not call out to the defenders.

He rose as silently as possible, though the bedsprings creaked, and tiptoed barefoot across to the door. The knob didn't budge when he tried to twist it. Not surprising. He decided it would be impossible to pick without any tools.

His gaze shifted to the windows. The center one had been left open a few inches, providing a cool breeze inside the overheated room. He crept over and peered outside. A grassy field surrounded the building, and beyond that, the thick concrete wall wrapped around the perimeter. Maybe that was considered sufficient defense from any of the initiates trying to escape. He didn't see any guards.

Acting quickly, he pushed the window higher, pulled himself onto the sill, and dropped to the ground outside. He crouched for a moment, looking around, making sure no one was in the vicinity. Then he stepped along the side of the building, moving down from the windows while keeping close to the fortress wall. He saw at once he would not be able to climb to the second floor unless he was lucky enough to find a sturdy drainage pipe. The place was constructed of smooth concrete, with not a handhold in sight.

He heard a quiet whistle and threw himself onto the ground, thinking it must be a sentry. But when he heard it again, it sounded like it was coming from above. He looked back in the other direction and saw her then. Ayva. Leaning from an open window, looking down at him.

Jarem scrambled to just below her window. "Forgive me," he whispered up to her.

"I understand why you had to volunteer," she said. "Jarem... I swear to you, I told no one about Fenn."

"I believe you."

"I wish I had... a different sort of father. One that would have helped."

"It only matters that you're not anything like him. Ayva, can you get out of your room and come down to me?"

THE TRIALS

"We're locked in here."

"Can you lower yourself from the window somehow? Is there anything you can use as a rope?"

"There isn't, but even if there was, what then?"

"We could run away."

She hesitated before shaking her head. "Defenders patrol the wall. I've seen them pass while I was watching here. Besides, I don't think you really mean it."

"I would do it for you. To help you escape."

"Now isn't the time. There needs to be a chance of success."

"We should've acted--"

"Hide!" she hissed, pulling back from the window.

Jarem dove to the ground and waited. He thought he heard voices in the distance, and then they drifted away. After a few minutes, Ayva returned. "They're gone now," she whispered.

He stood up and gazed at her beautiful face. The night was dark, but what he couldn't see he filled in from memory.

"What sort of defender will you be?" she asked.

"You mean, if I survive the Trials?"

"Shhh. Don't doubt yourself. You *will*. And then what sort of defender will you be?"

"The sort that questions everything."

"I don't know any like that."

"Then I'll be the first."

"Question things, yes," she said. "But not openly. Promise you'll do whatever it takes to stay alive."

"I'll do my best."

"Promise!"

"I promise," he said, meaning it yet knowing there might

be limits to what he might do to stay alive. "What sort of blest will you be?"

"Quiet and unassuming. The type no one notices. At the same time, I'll be watching. Noticing everything. Biding my time. Waiting for my moment to escape."

"You're going to escape?"

"Not right away. Not till you've sent word that you've come for me." She leaned lower, making him worry a bit that she might fall. "Jarem." Her voice soothed him. "Swear that you'll come for me after your ten years."

"But you won't be allowed to leave."

"I told you. I'll be planning my escape."

"Then I'll come for you."

Voices wafted toward them again, sounding closer now.

"I swear it," he whispered. "I won't rest until you're in my arms again."

"Be safe, my love." She drew back into her room before he could reply. He was relieved in a way. It made his heart ache to see her so near, when in reality, an enormous chasm separated them already.

He made it back to his bed without being observed, as far as he could tell. But sleep was elusive. After the sun revealed its first light above the horizon, he watched the two attendants arriving to take Kailo to the Trials.

"Good luck," Jarem whispered.

Kailo turned a blank face toward him before nodding curtly. The attendants left him with no time for hesitation as they hurried him from the room. Jarem was left feeling impressed by the boy's calm resolve.

During the rest of the day, Jarem was allowed to keep to the room. He drifted in and out of sleep, unable to find any position that didn't aggravate one or more of his injuries. When supper was announced, he forced himself to go to the

THE TRIALS

hall and eat as much as possible, because tomorrow was his day to compete.

At the end of the meal, they received the news that Kailo had died without completing the Trials. Time seemed to slow as Jarem scanned the faces of the others in their group, watching their eyes widening and their mouths gaping open in astonishment, just as his must have done. Of the twelve of them, Jarem would've voted Kailo most likely to succeed. It appeared they all had the same opinion.

Between the agony of his separation from Ayva, the self-doubt that Kailo's death awakened in him, and the continued pain resulting from his wounds, Jarem spent another sleepless night at a time when sleep was most needed. The room was still dark when he heard the door to their sleeping chamber coming open, and hard steps crossing the stone floor toward him.

35

I, ASTERIOS

The early sun painted the horizon a transcendent pink, and the sparrows tossed bright melodies between them on the morning they brought my Helena home.

When I caught her scent, I experienced a moment of pure elation. I pictured my daughter as I had seen her last, with the sun lighting her golden mane while her graceful form, quick with child, cantered across the pasture.

But my second breath of her brought with it the stench of death and decay. In my mind, I saw rotting flesh, bloody entrails, and maggots. It wasn't till then that I understood she was dead.

Fury rose up inside me. *What had the immortals done to her?* I would not let them keep me from her. I neighed my loudest, but no one came to let me out, not even Ethan. Then I bucked and kicked until the stall door broke open. I followed the odor to a large wagon in the pasture where she was laid out. The defenders who must've brought her home saw me galloping toward them and sprang back. No one dared get in my way.

I nuzzled her forehead and remained with my head pressed against hers for I'm not sure how long. If I were human and capable of tears, I could have filled a bucket with them.

At last, I raised my head and looked at her more closely. Undeniably, she had met with a violent death. Who or what could have done this to her? *And where was my grandchild?* I turned to the defenders, but none were speaking. Their faces were lowered, like they couldn't even bear to look at me. Or feared I might break their heads if I caught their gaze.

I took off across the pasture, bucking and flailing. I ran in circles, thinking I would lose my mind if the foal was dead too. When I finally had to stop for breath, I saw Apollo speaking with the stable master. A nearly irresistible urge filled me, to gallop toward Apollo and run him through with my horn. But he was immortal; his body would repair itself. I, on the other hand, would be killed by the defenders immediately.

First I wanted to know what happened.

I approached slowly, just close enough to hear him. He told Ethan that a grand ceremony in Olympus was being planned in her honor and that her body must be properly prepared for it. He went over some of the details before glancing toward me. "Asterios will lead the procession," he said.

If he thought that would placate me, he did not know me at all.

Apollo did not press his point, perhaps noticing the venom in my eyes for the first time. He left quickly with his defenders.

Ethan approached. I watched his measured gait and noted the hollow cheeks, the thick gray eyebrows, the sagging shoulders. Had he always looked this old and worn out? Or had the news of Helena's death shattered something inside him, as it had for me?

He brought me water. I drank thirstily while he leaned against the fence beside me. "She had the finest disposition of any horse I've known."

I whinnied in agreement. *Tell me about it.*

"It was a terrible mistake, what happened to her. Far as I can tell."

I looked hard at him to show him I understood. To show him I wanted the whole story.

He continued. "Zeus was beside himself when the boy Belic ran away. They say he stole an object of great value. So the immortal sent his most powerful weapon after him—a king eagle."

I made a sound like a growl.

"Ever seen one of those? Its wing span is wider than our stable roof. Claws the size of boulders." He looked at me. "If only it had a brain just as big."

Legend had it they were dumb as mud.

"Guess it decided a pregnant blest horse was more interesting prey than a scrawny mortal."

I kicked the back of the fence.

"The king eagle attacked her in the Skalbourne stable first. She broke out and ran into the forest. It got her there. Ate her entrails."

He could've spared me the details. *But what about the foal*, I was thinking. *Tell me about the foal.* I nudged his shoulder to show I wanted more.

"Aye, the foal," he said, reading my mind. "It's possible he ate the foal. But if so, he ate every bit of it, even the bones. Seems unlikely. Helena had much more succulent parts that he didn't touch. There was talk he might've carried the foal back to the nest. Don't think they've been able to reach the nest. But... this is interesting... some folks—immortals and mortals—saw the king eagle flying back to Olympus. Not one of them saw it carrying anything."

A spark of hope lit inside me.

"What I'm saying is that foal might still be alive. Maybe it ran away from the carnage and hid in the forest. Frightened out of its wits. If someone were to find the poor thing... there might still be a chance to save it."

He didn't look at me while he was saying this. As far as he knew, he was just talking to himself. Because who in their right mind would imagine a blest horse understanding mortal language?

36

RENNIE

The night following the Rite, Rennie dozed fitfully until waking just after midnight. She tried for another hour to go back to sleep, but her mind kept replaying the horrifying moment when Apollo laid his hand on Ayva's shoulder, until she couldn't bear to lie there a second longer.

She rose and crossed the hall to her sister's room, hearing her father's snores on the way. What was wrong with him? His daughter was virtually kidnapped, never to be seen or heard from again, and he happily slept. She would never understand how her mother could've married such a man.

After she shut the door behind her, a sudden weakness overwhelmed her. She leaned against the wall to steady herself. This room *was* Ayva, from the colors of the paint, the rug, and the bedspread, to the books and trinkets that lined her shelves, the intricate pencil drawings displayed on the walls, and the dresses hanging in her closet.

The blest weren't allowed to bring anything with them. Even the clothes they wore to the Rite would be taken away as soon as they changed into their new raiment. Nothing could be crueler than the spiriting away of initiates as soon as they were chosen. No kisses or embraces or murmured goodbyes. They were forbidden from keeping even a single physical remembrance from their former life. One day they were here, the next they were gone, never to be seen in Skalbourne again. It was exactly the same as if they'd died.

With renewed energy, Rennie swept around the room, examining everything. With each touch, memories flooded back to her. She had given Ayva the little smiling cat made of blue glass for her tenth birthday. But she'd loved it so much, the next day she stole it back and hid it in her room. Later, after she saw Ayva crying, thinking it was lost or broken, she secretly returned the trinket. It was a bitter irony to think, now that she could have it for herself, she would sacrifice this and any amount of wondrous treasures for Ayva to come home and never leave again.

She ran her hands over Ayva's bright-colored dresses. Her sister favored turquoise and yellow and red, colors that contrasted beautifully with her dark skin and black hair. Rennie, with her reddish locks and lighter skin tone, didn't think these colors flattered her at all, and in any case, she'd stopped wearing anything with a skirt years ago. She didn't know what they would do with all these lovely clothes, aside from leaving them here as a memorial to her absent sister.

On noticing the intricate wooden jewelry box Jarem had given Ayva for her sixteenth birthday, Rennie saddened again, thinking of what he and his family must be suffering. How would he even focus on completing the Trials with the specter of death hanging over his mother and brother? She wished she could pray hard for his success, but since she'd come to think of the immortals as the enemies of mortals, prayer was no longer an option for her.

Lying down on Ayva's bed, she wrapped the blanket around her, breathing in the floral scent of her sister that permeated the room. She lifted her hand and kissed the ring that had belonged to Ayva and their mother before that. When she closed her eyes, the tears slid from under her lids, along the sides of her face, getting lost in her hair.

"You've ruined us!" Poppa roared at Rennie, startling her awake.

She snapped into a sitting position, astonished to see her father looming over her with the front of his shirt stained in blood.

"Do you have any idea what you've done?"

"You're hurt, Poppa! Let me help you."

"If this gets out, we're ruined! Worse, we'll be sent to the gallows."

"I don't know what you mean. I'm sorry I slept in Ayva's room without asking."

"This isn't about Ayva! It's about the blest horse."

"Horse?" She put on her best *I'm innocent* face.

"You know what I'm talking about. The blest horse in the shed."

"In the...? It must've wandered in there."

"Don't lie to me! The horse nearly killed me!"

"What are you talking about?" Rennie knew Xander was as gentle as a lamb.

He pointed to his shirt. "Look at the blood!"

"Let me treat your wound, Poppa." But she noticed the shirt wasn't torn under the blood stain.

"It's the animal's blood, not mine."

"What have you done?"

"What have *I* done? Defended myself."

"Did you hurt him?" She jumped up and went to the window. "Where is he?"

"You're more worried about that thing than your own father. I heard noises in the shed and thought it was an intruder. I got a knife, and when I opened the door, the creature reared at me. It could've knocked me over!"

"But you said you weren't wounded."

"Because I slashed at it with my knife."

"You killed him!" Rennie rushed to the door.

"Would've been better if I had! Then you could've buried it and hidden the evidence. But it ran off!"

"We have to get him back!" Unlike her father, Rennie gave no thought to what might happen if Apollo learned she'd been harboring the missing blest colt. Instead, a powerful sensation of love and protectiveness for the horse overwhelmed her.

As she dashed outside, she heard Poppa shouting from the house, "Where do you think you're going?"

"I have to find him."

"Finish the job. Bury him before the immortals find out or you'll get us both hanged. And when you're done... I don't ever want to see you again."

Rennie didn't care what he said. She couldn't stand to think of Xander suffering alone out there, possibly dying. No matter what, she would try her best to save him.

37

FENN

The uproar began several hours after Fenn had fallen into a fitful sleep. Footsteps thumping on the front stoop. Fists pounding on the doors, front and back. Rocks banging against the side of the house. Voices hurling threats. "Death to the defective," "Blindie won't see what hurts him," "Come out, come out, Cadaver Eyes," and so much more.

When he'd walked home with the loremaster, Fenn had feared one of the ruffians might follow to see where he lived, and possibly return later with reinforcements. For this reason, he'd locked the shutters over the windows and bolted the doors before going to bed. *Thank the immortals.* Otherwise, they would've swarmed inside and almost certainly killed him.

The melee continued for several hours, devolving into complete drunken debauchery. Somebody beat on drums, another played a horn. People sang and laughed and whooped and hollered like they thought this was a game. The game of *Terrify the Blind Boy.*

Fenn huddled on a chair in the living room, covering his

ears. Their largest kitchen knife rested on the table beside him, in case anyone got in. It was probably useless, with so many of them and only one of him. If he stabbed quickly in all directions, maybe he could hold them off briefly, but sooner or later, they'd wrench the weapon from his hand and use it against him. Nevertheless, its presence gave him a modicum of comfort.

When the noises died down and drifted away, he returned to bed, but wasn't able to settle his nerves enough to sleep. Each new sound put him on alert again, as he strained his hearing to decipher if it represented a new threat.

As dawn approached, his thoughts turned to Mother. He went into her room and lay down on her bed. At this very moment, they could be fitting the noose around her neck. He knew she would be thankful neither of her sons were being prepared for execution beside her. His mother had an inner strength that had given her the power to defy the gods. She would face her death with a brave acceptance of the inevitable. It came to him she had always been the cement that kept their family resilient. Without her, without his brother, he felt the will to live slipping away from him.

He turned his face to the pillow and wept.

Much later, after the sun had risen, a knock at the door startled him. He made no movement, thinking it must be more troublemakers from town, until a boy shouted from outside. "Are you home, Fenn? I'm Kern, the loremaster's assistant. He asked me to call on you and see if you needed anything."

Fenn dragged himself from the bed and went to the door. "Are you alone?" he asked.

"Yes," the boy answered.

Fenn believed him, because the child had known his

name and spoken in a civil manner. He let Kern into the house.

"I'm sorry for what happened," the boy said.

"You know about it?"

"I saw it. Outside. Have you been...? Oh, sorry, I guess you wouldn't have seen it."

"What do you mean?"

"There are words painted all over your house."

"Words?"

"Well, mainly just one word, repeated."

"What word?"

"I'd rather not say. It isn't nice."

"I suppose it was 'defective.'"

"Sorry. And it looks like they stomped all over your garden. People can be cruel sometimes."

"I'm learning that."

"Can I bring you anything to eat?"

After everything that had happened, Fenn had no appetite. "That's okay."

"The loremaster will be upset with me if I don't get you anything."

"Whatever you want, then," Fenn said. "Let me get you the money."

"He also insisted on paying this time."

Fenn did not have the energy to argue. "That's really kind of him."

"May I ask you something?" Kern said.

"All right."

"Can you see anything at all?"

"No."

"It's all black for you?"

"I don't know what you would call it. I don't know what *black* looks like."

"That's interesting. And the way your eyes appear all whitish. You know? Or maybe you don't. I suppose *white* means no more than *black* to you."

"That's true. But I know my eyes are white because that's what my mother and brother told me."

"Were they always like this?"

"I think they got whiter over the first few years of my life. My mother said so, anyway."

"Is there a chance you'll ever see again?"

"I can't imagine how."

"It must be hard for you," Kern said.

"The hardest thing is the judgment of others."

"Sorry. I'll get your food now. Thank you for answering my questions."

"You seem very curious for your age."

"The loremaster tells me curiosity is how we learn about the world. And that learning is the key to all knowledge. I should be back soon. Would you like me to use a secret knock so you won't confuse me with whoever messed up your house?"

Fenn laughed. What a difference a conversation with someone kind could make. "Just call for me through the door and that will work. Or make up a special code, if you prefer."

Kern knocked twice slowly, and three times fast on his return, and left after dropping off the items. Fenn put away the food before going out to check the traps. Though there was still brined meat in the barrel in case his appetite returned, he hated the thought of a terrified animal waiting in the trap for a long time. It reminded him of his own experience cowering inside the house last night.

Mother and Jarem had set up a network of string tied between trees, allowing Fenn to find his way to each trap. He heard movement as he drew close to the first one. But before he could check the trap, another sound caught his ear—the whinny of a horse. But the sound was weak, like the animal might be young, or in distress.

Fenn loved animals, though he had no experience of horses. From the age of four until six months ago, he'd had a dog. When Rusty died, Mother said they couldn't get another until after the Rite. The dog had slept in his bed and often helped lead him around the house, inside and out. Just thinking about Rusty's passing caused a river of emotions to rush through him.

"Hey there," he said to the horse. Its plaintive cry continued.

"Is your mom around?" If it was a foal or a yearling, its mother ought to be nearby. But he could hear no sounds of it.

Fenn reached out and felt around till his hands touched the animal where it was lying on the ground. Its flank trembled.

"It's okay, baby." He caressed its side, deciding it could be a yearling but no older than that. "What's wrong? Where's your mama?"

His hand moved up the horse's neck until he felt something sticky. When he lowered his face to it, he smelled blood. "What happened to you?"

The foal's breathing was labored. Fenn touched the bloody area and discerned what felt like the smooth cut of a knife. "Who would do a thing like this?"

That's when it came to him. The ruffians who'd surrounded his house last night. They would be just the sort to wound an innocent creature and leave it lying in pain and misery as the life force ebbed out of it. Likely they killed the foal's mother too. *Bastards.*

He reached underneath and tried to lift it, but the horse was heavy, at least a hundred pounds. Its mother must've been quite large. He didn't think he could carry the foal all the way back to the house, certainly not in a comfortable position. The wagon would be necessary.

"I'll be back soon," he said before winding his way rapidly along the path. He returned not only with the wagon, but also the supplies to dress the wound. It would be safer to do that before transporting the foal, he thought.

He'd stitched quite a few cuts before, beginning with the time Mother slashed herself with broken glass when Jarem wasn't home. He murmured tender words of comfort to the foal as he worked on it, and the patient kept calm, as if it understood it would feel much better in the end.

By the time he finished, Fenn discovered two more things about the horse. First, that it was male. The second, that the upper bridge of its nose sported the stub of a horn.

Only blest horses had horns. So his brother had told him. And *only immortals were permitted to touch blest horses.*

Fenn loaded the colt onto his wagon and drew him back to the house. It didn't matter the consequences. He would not leave this poor wounded creature outside to die alone in the dark.

38

AYVA

The morning after Ayva and Jarem said their goodbyes, she and the other two chosen to be blest were allowed to bathe and change into the clothing worn by initiates. For Ayva and Katreen, this meant undyed linen skirts that fell to their ankles and white blouses with low necklines. Joss received a white tunic and plain linen trousers.

They were fed a satisfying breakfast before being escorted outside to a carriage drawn by two sturdy horses. The handsome young man who opened the door for Ayva smiled at her, but she lowered her eyes while climbing inside and settling on the plush seat. Joss sat beside her, while Katreen took the place across, facing opposite the direction they would be traveling.

"I hope I won't get an upset stomach facing this way," Katreen said.

"You can take my seat," Ayva said.

"No, this is fine. I'm sure I'll get used to it."

Ayva did not insist. Her impression so far was that

Katreen was happiest when she had something to suffer over.

As the carriage moved, a flood of emotion brought tears to Ayva's eyes, despite her resolve to remain strong and not think of Jarem.

"Just look at the two of you," Katreen said. "Don't you know how lucky we are?"

Joss blew his nose with a handkerchief. "I don't know how my grandmother will manage without me. I'm her only grandchild, and my parents are dead. She forgets things all the time."

"I'm worried about my father and sister," Ayva said.

"What about the boy you spoke to out the window last night?" Katreen said.

Ayva's cheeks grew hot. She hadn't realized Katreen was awake. "I'll miss him too," Ayva said.

"It's a shame you formed an attachment. I never did. I decided I should wait till after the Rite. I didn't want my heart to be broken if I was picked."

"Lucky for you to have a heart so easily controlled," Joss said. "What about your family? You're not sad to leave them?"

"Not really. I have lots of younger sisters and brothers. I'm happy not to have to help care for them anymore."

"Instead, we'll be caring for the immortals." Ayva hoped that didn't sound like a complaint.

"Blessed are the caretakers," Joss murmured.

Silence fell over them as they all returned to looking out the windows. Ayva tried not to think about what she was leaving behind, and instead to focus on the future that awaited her. Since she had never left home before, her thoughts tingled to see how other people lived. Wide swathes of farmland filled the area to the east of Skalbourne, between the town and the foothills. Corn and grain and cotton appeared to be the major crops, though she also spotted lettuce, tomatoes, squash, and other summer vegetables in several of the fields.

At one point, the carriage passed close to a group of workers harvesting corn. They were covered in so much sweat, she thought at first they'd been doused in water. Despite their apparent exhaustion, they moved among the stalks, picking rapidly. Some of them looked to be no more than eleven or twelve years old. Two defenders watched the group, and when one child paused briefly to wipe his forehead, a defender shoved him back toward the stalks.

Ayva had heard that the immortals owned the farmland surrounding Olympus, but had not imagined they monitored the farm workers with armed defenders. Working conditions appeared brutal.

Later they passed a group of shacks roughly constructed and in need of repair. Seeing clothes hung out on lines, she realized with a shock that these were homes for the workers. The ground was nothing but dirt, unlike most Skalbourne residences, which had lush yards filled with trees and flowers. A girl of about eight, with mussed hair and a smudged face, caught Ayva's eye as the carriage rolled by. Her blank-faced stare spoke of misery and hardship.

Moments later, the carriage halted abruptly.

"Why are we stopping here?" Katreen asked, craning her head around to get a look.

"Someone's been hurt!" a man shouted, running past them up the road.

Ayva's natural instinct to be of service drew her out of the carriage.

"Wait!" Katreen shouted. "You can't get out! It's not allowed."

Ayva ignored her and followed their driver, who had already climbed down and was walking toward where a crowd had gathered up ahead in the middle of the lane.

To her astonishment, Ares—looming taller than any of the mortals surrounding him—stood at the center beside his blest horse. His retinue of defenders was busy trying to establish order among the villagers.

Ayva paused, her stomach churning at her last memory of the immortal. She forced the image of his bloody chin out of her mind. *It wasn't real,* she told herself. *It could not have been real.*

"What happened here?" the driver asked a woman with a mud-splattered skirt and a frozen expression.

"Ma'am, are you all right?" he said when she didn't respond.

The woman shook herself. "The boy... it were Ned, I think. Ran out in front of the blest horse. Horse couldn't stop. Boy got trampled."

"Ned didn't see them coming?" the driver said.

"Aye," the woman said. "I think he did."

Ayva shivered. She wondered if the child thought that being killed by an immortal might bring him closer to the divine.

The crowd dispersed after the boy's body was taken away. Ayva was about to return to the carriage when she noticed Ares had moved closer to where she stood. He was speaking to one of his defenders, but his eyes were on her. When he saw her returning his gaze, he gave a slight nod of his head.

Flustered, she swiveled and hastened back to the carriage. She told herself she had to have mistaken his intent. He must have been nodding at someone else behind her. It was impossible she could've attracted the interest of any immortal, let alone that one, who was known far and wide for his surly disposition.

But before the carriage started up again, Ares rode his horse up to the driver and spoke with him.

"Look who it is!" Katreen hissed.

Ayva heard the driver saying something about taking the new blest to Kenton Fortress.

Ares moved on, followed by his defenders.

"I wonder what that was about," Joss said.

Ayva felt her short hair, reminding herself how Rennie had chopped it up. No one could find her beautiful now, especially not an immortal. Whatever intent Ares had in speaking to the driver, it could not have had anything to do with her.

39

AYVA

It was not long after the tragic death of the child that their carriage left the fields behind and ascended toward Olympus along a series of switchbacks.

"It's steeper than I imagined," Joss said.

"Have you never seen it before?" Katreen asked.

He shook his head.

"I haven't either," Ayva said.

"I've made the trip to Olympus several times with my father. It's quite incredible."

Ayva wondered if she was telling the truth, but didn't care enough to challenge her statement. A short while later, the carriage stopped moving. They had come to the entrance of another fortress, similar in design to where they had spent the last night, though this one was taller and stretched farther from end to end.

"I suppose we'll get some refreshment here," Katreen said.

A defender ushered them out of the carriage. "Follow me." He led them across a central hall with sentries posted all around, to a small waiting area with a padded bench next to a door. "You're to remain here until you're called."

"For how long?" Katreen said.

"Until you're called."

"I mean, when will we be continuing to Olympus?"

"Not till your training is complete."

"How long will that take?"

"I wouldn't know. Good luck." The defender rushed away before Katreen could hurl more questions at him.

It wasn't what any of them had expected. Ayva had consoled herself with the thought of seeing Olympus right away. Its beauty and splendor were legendary. She'd thought the excitement of exploring it would distract her from the pain of leaving Jarem behind. But now they'd have to wait for who knew how long.

Sighing, Joss sat on the bench.

"I'm not sure I would do that if I were you," Katreen said. "It may not be allowed."

"Sitting?"

"Sitting here. Without permission."

He frowned and stood back up.

"I'll take my chances." Ayva settled onto the bench. "I wonder how many initiates have waited here just like us."

"Thousands." Katreen spoke with assurance. "We should speak more quietly."

Joss sat back on the bench next to Ayva while Katreen continued standing. It wasn't long before the door came open and a man and woman dressed in the manner of the blest stepped out.

"Katreen?" the woman asked.

"I'm Katreen."

"Come with me."

"And you come with me," the man told Joss.

"Should I come too?" Ayva asked as they stepped away.

"No," the woman said.

There seemed to be a limit on conversation here, Ayva thought as she was left alone in the hall. Answers came in the form of nothing beyond strictly necessary information. She hugged herself, trying to calm her nerves. *If only they hadn't picked me*, she thought. *If only I were back home with Jarem, and he hadn't volunteered. If only we could make a life together without any of this nonsense.* Then she glanced around nervously, wondering if the immortals were more likely to hear her thoughts now that she was closer to Olympus.

The door opened and another blest approached. She looked to be in her thirties and gazed at Ayva with dull, glazed eyes. Her face showed no expression.

"I'm Blest Iris," she said. "You are to come with me."

Ayva stood up, thinking this woman looked familiar to her, but she couldn't recall knowing anyone named Iris. She followed the woman into a corridor, down a flight of steps and along another hallway, until they passed through a door leading outside. On a small patio made more private by three surrounding walls, there was a single chair and a coal fire burning in a cast-iron stove. An iron rod stuck out from it.

"Sit down," Blest Iris said. "Before we begin, you must learn the first, most important rule. You are to forget everything about your past and never speak of it. Not your friends, not your family, not the town where you grew up. Not even your own name. Think of today as the day you were born. Your name is Blest Raven. It was, is, and will be Blest Raven forever more."

Ayva struggled to hold back tears. No matter what Iris told her, she would never forget Jarem or Rennie or her mother or even her father. She would not speak of them, but she would hold their memories close inside her heart. "Yes, Blest Iris," she said.

"Good. Now remove your clothing above the waist."

"I don't understand." Ayva looked across the courtyard, nervous that someone might be watching, though she couldn't see anyone. "Am I changing my clothes?"

"No. I'm going to give you the mark we proudly wear." Blest Iris said this in a voice without inflection. She lowered the top of her blouse to show Ayva the outline of a goblet seared into her flesh on the upper part of her right breast.

An icy sensation filled Ayva and froze her blood. "Is that a branding? Like, for animals?"

"Yes."

Her eyes flicked madly to the iron rod in the fire. "You're using that on me?"

"It only takes a second. There are worse things."

Ayva couldn't imagine anything worse. "Why must we have this cup on our breasts?"

"Because we're the cupbearers. The cup is our symbol. The sign that we're blest now and forever."

To Ayva, that seemed like a hidden way of saying, once you're branded, you cannot escape. It will always be possible to identify you as blest.

"Please don't do it. I beg you. You... you look so familiar. Do you have a sister? I think her name is Fiona. She and my mother were dear friends."

Blest Iris stared at her in surprise. "You know Fiona?" she whispered.

"Yes. I could tell you some things about her."

"Never mention her. I told you, we're forbidden to speak of the past. If you forget again, there will be consequences!"

Her gaze shifted back to the iron rod. "We must do this now."

"I want to go back." Ayva was aware she sounded hysterical. "I don't want to be a blest. I don't want that foul thing on my breast."

"You can cooperate," Blest Iris said, "Or four Defenders will hold you down. Either way, you will end up with the branding."

Ayva shook all over. Being held down with four defenders viewing her nakedness would only make the torture worse. There was nothing she could do, no way to escape from a building crawling with sentries. She removed her blouse and undergarment and closed her eyes. "Do it."

She felt the searing heat of the red hot iron coming for her.

40

JAREM

At dawn on the day he was to undergo the Trials, Jarem rose with a clenched stomach and a bitter taste in the back of his throat. He was taken to an early breakfast, where he swallowed as much food as he could manage despite a complete lack of hunger. He needed every bit of strength and stamina it might give him.

After the meal, the guards escorted him to a private audience with someone who called himself a physician. However, the doctor did not perform any kind of an examination on him, nor even comment on his wounded condition. He simply handed Jarem a small cup of a purple liquid to drink. "Everyone drinks it," he said. "It gives you a little confidence boost. Helps to quell the nerves."

As it didn't seem optional, Jarem swallowed it without argument. The potion tasted bitter with a touch of sweetness, as if sugar had been added to cover the bad flavor.

They told him he could bring nothing but the clothes on his back. When he'd gone home briefly before the Rite, he had thought to grab a coil of rope and to wrap it through the loops on his trousers in lieu

THE TRIALS

of a belt. One never knew when a rope might be helpful. But after a defender noticed it, he was told to remove it.

Two men rode in the carriage with him for a journey that led up into the mountains. Neither of them spoke; Jarem's one attempt to engage them in conversation met with deaf ears.

His hands prickled with anticipation while his insides churned. What chance did any of them have if someone as powerful and well-trained as Kailo—built-like-a-bear Kailo—had failed? Jarem had felt his confidence erode in the hours following the announcement of the boy's death.

Roughly two hours after they departed, the terrain leveled out, and the carriage arrived at a wooden cabin that marked the start of the course. Captain Broyland emerged from the doorway to greet him. "Good morning, Jarem. I hope you're ready to face the Trials today."

"Yes, sir."

"Two things before you start. The course is marked by blue rope strung on both sides. If you cross beyond the rope on either side, you have lost and you will forfeit your life. You must always stay within the bounds of the ropes.

"Secondly, if you do not reach the end of the course by sunset, you will forfeit your life. Do you understand?"

"Yes, sir."

"These are the only rules."

Jarem drank water that was offered to him before following the captain to a path bound by the ropes. "Get ready," the captain said.

Jarem took his place at the starting line.

"I wish you success." Captain Broyland sounded sincere. "Ready..."

Jarem's muscles tensed.

"Set... Go!" Fireworks shot up with a resounding explosion and lit the sky with streaks of blue and red.

Jarem felt his legs moving. It was unreal, this thing he'd imagined all his life, and now he was here, dashing along this path, wishing this was all there was to it, a race from beginning to end with no other complications. But if that were the case, Kailo would still be alive.

The sun glared down at him from a cloudless sky, making him appreciate the cool relief when the trail plunged into deep woods. But the shadows increased the likelihood of his not seeing a hazard in time. He might fall into a hidden pit, or step on a trap that would snap his ankle, or get lifted upside down by a rope snare. Animals might suddenly appear and attack him. They were told nothing about what they would face in the Trials; he could only imagine the worst.

Time passed before he came out from the forest and into a wide plain. An enormous raised structure lay ahead; from its shape, he guessed it was a theater or stadium of some sort. His nerves tingled inside him, wondering what it might hold. The blue ropes led him to an open door at the base of the structure; he had no choice but to enter without having any idea what might be inside.

Steps took him downward, and then he followed a dark corridor leading to a closed door. Could the thing that killed Kailo be on the other side? Regardless, he must face it, and any hesitation would just cost him time. He flung open the door.

The sunshine dazzled him after the dimness of the stairs. He blinked, momentarily blinded. As his vision returned, he saw he was in an enormous empty arena. Flags bearing the standard of the immortals—five linked rings in the same shade of blue that wrapped their wrists and necks

THE TRIALS

—waved along the perimeter. High above, there were rows partly veiled. He glimpsed the shadows of people seated, observing him. Voices murmured. They had to be immortals, since mortals weren't allowed to view the Trials. He supposed they must have their entertainment.

The door banged shut behind him as his eyes shifted to survey the arena. Across and to the side, something covered in tarp lay on the ground. From the shape, it looked as if it could be a smallish person. He was about to move toward it when he spotted an open doorway in the wall opposite his own position.Without hesitation, he raced toward it, figuring he would soon have good reason to exit this stadium.

In that same instant, a huge metal gate set into the wall, so big he hadn't realized it was a gate, rolled open. Thunderous footsteps and a loud clanging preceded the entrance of a cyclops. The giant—nearly three times Jarem's height—planted his massive foot in the boy's direction.

Jarem slid to a stop and gaped at the creature in disbelief. He knew the story of Odysseus, but had never imagined the one-eyed giants to be real. The massive chest of the cyclops was bare, and he had a cloth wrapped around his private areas below. His long hair was tied behind his back, while the strands of his beard hung like tangled vines down from his chin. His eye glowed green. But most importantly, the cyclops clutched a huge wooden club between his gnarled hands.

Shock kept Jarem frozen in place for too long. The cyclops raised his club and brought it down to squash the mortal like a fly. Almost too late, Jarem leapt sideways, avoiding certain death by a matter of inches. He barely had time to spring back to his feet before the club was coming toward him again. He saved himself with another dive, and then two more after that. But he was slowing down, becoming exhausted, and he knew he wouldn't last much longer.

At least the cyclops appeared to be slowing, too. Jarem caught a second to look around and discover that the sound of metal clanging came from thick chains attached to the giant's ankles. It could only mean there was a limit to how far the cyclops could go in the arena. Armed with this supposition, he bolted in the opposite direction from where the giant had emerged. Mammoth steps that shook the whole stadium crashed behind him, and he knew the next blow was imminent. His lungs were near to bursting as he raced to the wall. If his theory was wrong, he was a dead man.

The club landed a foot behind Jarem, who turned to see the cyclops pulling furiously at his restraints. The creature exploded with a roar of frustration.

Jarem leaned against the wall and caught his breath. Again he scanned the arena and saw that if he moved toward the door he'd noticed earlier, hugging the wall, he had a chance of reaching it while keeping outside the reach of the cyclops.

"Forgetting something?"

The loud, rumbling tone came from the giant. Jarem paused and looked at him in surprise. He had assumed the cyclops couldn't talk.

The cyclops laughed with a deep bellow, revealing jagged yellow teeth. "Thought I was stupid, didn't you?"

"I assumed you were very smart," Jarem protested, "But too busy trying to kill me to have time for conversation. What did I forget?"

The cyclops reached down and pulled the tarp off the bundle curled up on the ground. Horror filled Jarem to see his mother lying there, unconscious or dead. He ran toward her, but seeing the giant lift his club, he forced himself to draw back. "What have you done to her?!" he screamed.

"Nothing," the cyclops said. "Yet."

Jarem's eyes shot from side to side, desperately seeking a weapon to use against the monster.

"You can save her," the cyclops said. "I'll take you for her."

"And then you'll kill me."

The cyclops shrugged. "It's what I do."

In all the training Jarem had done to prepare, no part of it had involved having to give up the life of someone he loved more than himself in order to survive the Trials. Was he meant to somehow save both of them? He'd been planning on skirting the reach of the monster to avoid confrontation, and now this was no longer an option.

"You don't get time to think about it." The cyclops raised his club over Mother's prostrate form.

"WAIT!" Jarem bellowed, his mind racing. "Do you swear not to harm her if I give myself over to you?"

"Said I'd take you for her. Not up to me. Those are the rules."

Jarem thought he must be telling the truth, but still he hesitated, desperately trying to devise a solution. While he racked his brain, an eagle flew down from the top of the arena and circled above the giant's head before gliding past Jarem and disappearing out of the open doorway to the outside.

The cyclops raised the club higher, ready to strike Jarem's mother.

"STOP! All right, I'll give myself up."

"Come here," the giant said, "Or watch me crush every bone in her body."

Jarem surveyed the arena once more, looking for

anything that might be useful, praying for an idea. This time, he noticed a pile of small stones by the wall. Picking up a handful, he approached the edge of the boundary where he was still safe from the giant's reach. He hurled a stone toward his eye, but it fell short, landing on the chin instead. The creature laughed. "Stupid mortal thinks he can hurt me with a pebble." He laughed some more. "Can't even feel it."

Jarem stepped nearer, testing the edge of the boundary, and threw a second rock, which hit the giant's cheek. He inched closer and hurled a third, which bounced off his eyelid, but it only made the cyclops double over with laughter. "Oh my immortals, he thinks he can blind me with a piece of dust. Odysseus had a thick spear, stupid. You know nothing!"

One more step and Jarem raised his arm to throw again. But his opponent, seeing he was now within the boundary, raised his club and slammed it down.

Jarem spun sideways, and just as quickly, as soon as the club landed, he jumped onto it and scrambled up the giant's arm like a fast-moving spider. The cyclops dropped the club and tried to grab him, but by then he had reached the neck. He leapt to the back side, grabbing onto the giant's hair, using it like a rope swing to propel himself to his quarry. He let go and flung out his arms, saying a prayer inside his head. Grasping the flagpole he'd been aiming for, the wood bent under his weight and for a precious second his thoughts plunged in agony, thinking he'd failed. Then he heard the wood snap.

He and the wood dropped hard to the stone floor of the stadium. Jarem lost hold of the pole, which turned out to be for the best. The cyclops, unaware of his intent, turned, and with a terrifying grin of satisfaction, leaned toward him to pick him up. Just as he was bent at his lowest, Jarem rolled and snatched up the flagpole, turning it so the sharp, jagged end that had broken off faced the giant, and thrust it with all his strength into the one enormous eye.

The monster wailed and clapped his hands over the bleeding hole where his eye had been. Jarem wasted no time in snatching up his mother and running with her toward the door at the far end. The cyclops roared in pain and fury. Mere seconds passed before his rage drove him to raise his club again and smash it down again and again. The second blow nearly got them, but then the cyclops got confused about their direction, and likely couldn't hear them over his own furious cries, allowing Jarem to reach the door. Applause came from the stands above. Jarem looked up and waved one hand in victory before whisking Mother out of the arena alive.

Outside, no sooner had he laid her down than two defenders appeared and pushed him away from her. "She'll be all right," was all they would say, but it was enough. He watched a moment longer as one of them carried her toward the back of the arena, where a whirl of dust blew up and surrounded them. When the dust settled, he could no longer see his mother in the man's arms. But he had no time to ponder whether she disappeared into thin air, or if his mind was playing tricks on him. The Trials must be completed before day's end.

41

JAREM

Judging from the angle of the sun, it was mid-afternoon by the time Jarem approached an expansive lake along a path lined with purple flowers that gave off the most exquisite scent. He'd never seen or smelled anything quite like them, he thought, as he sucked in the aroma. For a moment, they made him feel lightheaded and even a little dizzy, but he felt better once he moved past them toward the edge of the water, where a small boat equipped with oars awaited him.

From what he could see, the blue rope surrounded the lake, meaning anywhere on the water would be within bounds. On the shore directly across from where he stood, he could make out some sort of scaffolding painted the same blue as the rope. Despite having the entire body of water as his playground, he obviously needed to set out in that direction as quickly as possible.

He removed his shoes to walk into the water, pushing the boat out. The sand felt slimy to his feet, and the reed grass thickened and grew more clingy with each step. The murky color kept him from seeing more than a foot beneath the surface. He quivered inside, remembering the stories of giant serpents living in the depths of distant lakes that he and his friends would tell. As quickly as possible, he climbed in and took up the oars.

Rowing was one of the many skills he'd practiced in preparing for the Trials, and he might've enjoyed it now if he wasn't racing for his life. The air was still, and the lake's surface, smooth and glassy. He pulled at a steady pace, feeling confident about his odds of reaching the other side in good time.

A sound came from the distance. A clear, pure, silken note. The sound expanded and grew louder until he recognized it as the voices of women singing. He glimpsed them then, three young women on the starboard shore. Their looks were as bewitching as their silvery tone. They wore blue gowns to match the color of the immortals. But the material was light and nearly transparent, so that their perfectly formed bodies could be seen through the dresses. The women struck him as the most entrancing females he had ever encountered, even more exquisite than Ayva, who he loved.

He couldn't discern the lyrics of their mesmerizing song, yet it conveyed this message inside his head: *Come here, handsome rower. Come here and we will give you your heart's desire.*

Their voices awakened an irresistible craving inside him. He yearned for their warm hands to caress his body and their soft lips to kiss him. Without realizing, he had changed his direction and was rowing toward them.

But some tiny part of him remembered why he was here. Remembered that the first challenge was the cyclops, and this, then, must be the sirens. What had he read about them? That their seductive melody would lure a man to his death?

Still, he kept moving toward them, drawing closer and closer, unable to make himself turn away. How had Odysseus and his men made it past them? Odysseus had been bound to the mast while his men had their ears plugged.

Though he couldn't change direction, he forced himself to lay down his oars long enough to slash two small pieces from his shirt and push them hard into his ears. But he could still hear them; he swore they must've raised their voices. The desire to touch their silken skin overwhelmed him. He rowed closer.

Just as he'd almost reached them, their hands stretched out to grasp the bow of the boat and pull it toward them. In that second, when they thought they were victorious, they let down their guard, and he saw them for what they were. Hideous creatures with fishlike faces, scaled skin, webbed fingers, and long yellow claws that scratched at the boat.

He scrabbled to the stern and dove out. Swimming underwater, he didn't surface until his lungs were near bursting. They had resumed their singing, but the water distorted the sound and kept it from having the same effect. When he came up for air, he rolled onto his back to keep his ears submerged while he snatched a breath before diving under again. Another minute passed before the singing stopped.

The test must've ended since he'd found a way to defeat it. He regretted it was over because his body still itched for that sensation of exquisite torture. But he swam his fastest and was gratified to see he would soon be at the opposite shore.

Something brushed against his foot and made him jerk away and increase his pace. Probably just a fish, though he pictured the sirens in their true guise. Webbed fingers, fish-like faces...

Something banged against his thigh. Jarem kicked out in that direction and stroked harder. He hated how the cloudy water kept him from seeing anything.

A clawed hand lunged out of the water and grasped his shoulder, pulling him down. He struggled to shake her off, but her grip was like iron. Her head with scaled skin and reed grass hair rose beside him. "Save me," she said in a raspy voice, nothing like the sweet tones he'd heard.

She pulled him under with both hands and held him down. At the last second, he broke away, surfaced, and sucked in air. Then the siren was back, grappling to get him under again.

Jarem fought back, punching the side of her head. After three blows, she went limp. He held her face under the water, wondering if he should drown her to keep her from attacking again. After all, she'd tried to kill him. Of course, she might not even be capable of drowning.

He'd had enough of these creatures. He pushed her away and swam toward shore. But he couldn't help thinking she too might be subject to the immortals' whims. Maybe she was forced to swim out here to challenge him. Maybe she didn't deserve to die.

Cursing himself, he turned back and dove under the water, feeling around for her, wondering if she'd sunk to the bottom and he was already too late. But then he found her, still limp, still sinking. He wrapped his arm around her neck, drew her to the surface, and brought her to shore.

She sat up, spat, and took a deep breath. "*Fool*," she said in her raspy voice. She returned to the lake and disappeared back under the water.

He had no time to ponder her meaning. The sun was low on the horizon now. He ran.

42

JAREM

He prayed he was nearing the end as the terrain became rockier. Large slabs leaned against each other like the immortals had placed them in a giant game of dominoes. But his direction continued to be clearly laid out by the blue ropes.

Jarem heard the creature before rounding the bend and coming upon the thing he'd feared since leaving the sirens. Scylla and Charybdis, or at least Scylla. Ahead, the path diverged into two. The monstrous beast that was Scylla filled the passage on the left, her six lizard heads waving wildly on long snakelike necks in their frenzy to attack. Each open mouth panted to tear into his flesh and bone with knife-edged teeth.

It only took one to see him and cause all the heads to whip around and face him. The mouths drooled and the throats screeched. Two snapped at each other like they were vying to be first to rip out his throat.

A chain held Scylla to the rock wall beside her. But since she reached from there to the rope on her other side, there was no way to squeeze around her as he'd done with the cyclops. The only way past her would be to slay her.

Complicating matters were the words carved into the stone beside her: *In Immortals We Trust.* Was this meant to mislead him?

He had no knife, but what did it matter? By the time he might hack off one head, five others would be shredding him with their teeth. He did a rapid search of the area in case someone had been thoughtful enough to leave something useful, like a sword or hatchet. But there was nothing he could use as a weapon, not even a pile of rocks to hurl at her.

He turned his attention to the path on the right. Its first part appeared empty, with no obvious dangers to block his passage. But then the path disappeared from view behind another section of large boulders. He assumed the paths must eventually rejoin beyond Scylla, but there was no way to be sure. Jarem knew that in the story, Odysseus had to choose between crossing within reach of Scylla or through the domain of Charybdis. There had been no harmless option.

Charybdis was an ocean whirlpool with the power to swallow entire ships. The immortals had advised Odysseus that Scylla was the safer option. Of course, there was no ocean here, but maybe there was some sort of whirlpool beyond the boulders.

Other possibilities had to be considered. Were the words *In Immortals We Trust* to be taken as a command from them to follow that direction? If so, why didn't they say it more directly? *The immortals say, choose this path or die.* There was no ambiguity in that.

On the other hand, this could be a test of his intelligence. What fool would take a path blocked by a six-headed demon when there was a reasonably safe-looking one right next to it?

With time running out, he knew he must act. He thought he might be able to glimpse whatever dangers lay behind the rocks if he walked down the path a short way. After that, he could make his final decision about the route.

He took a cautious step that seemed safe, and then another. The ground below his foot felt oddly soft and sandy, but he was careful to test it for support before putting his weight on the forward foot. He continued like this for ten or twelve more feet, when suddenly the ground beneath him swirled. He tried to back away from it, but the shifting sand threw him off balance. He fell down as a hole grew beneath him. Slipping further and further downward, he threw his arms out, grasping frantically for a handhold.

"Help!" he called out, though he knew there was no help in the Trials.

He dropped deeper and deeper into the hole until it opened into a wide emptiness below him. He plummeted downward, with nothing but darkness all around.

43

RENNIE

The day before, Rennie had spent hours searching for Xander without finding him. How far could a wounded colt go? The thought that he might've lain down at the base of some tree and burrowed under a pile of leaves to die broke her heart. She couldn't stand to think of him feeling alone and unloved, cut with a knife for no reason whatsoever and forsaken by his mother (again). But she didn't know where else to look for him. She could only hope he had made it back to the immortals somehow, or to someone who'd returned him to the immortals, and that, at this very moment, they were nursing him back to health. Poppa had been right about one thing; she had been selfish to insist on keeping him as her own.

During the hours spent searching for Xander, she came to a decision. Poppa had told her he never wanted to see her again. Whether or not he really meant it, she was done with him. Not just him, but all of Skalbourne. She'd heard rumors of a band of heretics hiding out in the Savagelands. She dreamed of running away and joining them in a revolt against the tyranny of the immortals. Together they would free Ayva and all the other blest.

Rennie snuck into the house after dark and was glad to find that Poppa had not returned. She knew there was a certain widow who appealed to him, and who he often visited in the evenings. No doubt he went to stay with her rather than take the chance the immortals might show up to claim their horse that he might've killed. She snorted to herself and went to sleep in Ayva's room in the hope he wouldn't check there if he decided to come back during the night.

She needed money to pay for her trip, and she knew how to get it. In the morning, after verifying Poppa had still not come home, she gathered all the clothing and baubles that belonged to Ayva and put them in boxes to bring to the market for sale. Her sister would never need them again, and Rennie would never use them. She didn't plan to ask Poppa for permission. As far as she knew, he had not entered Ayva's room since the Rite, possibly because he didn't want to be reminded that he might actually miss her. With luck, she would be well on her way out of Skalbourne before Poppa discovered Ayva's room had been stripped bare.

Rennie tracked down Teddy, whose father grew vegetables, and hired him to deliver her boxes to the market via horse and cart. She squeezed herself and her wares in between the glass blower and the potter. At first they didn't want to share the space, but Ayva's pretty dresses changed their minds. Sure enough, the clothes drew attention and brought more shoppers to their section.

Her items were selling out quickly, in large part because she did very little haggling for better prices. She was a rather poor salesperson, which might be something to keep in mind when it came time for her to find actual employment. Whenever someone became excited over any of the dresses, or the delicate little figurines, or the silver earrings, Rennie couldn't keep herself from letting the item go for however little the customer was able to pay. It meant everything to her that the things Ayva loved would continue to be cherished by the new owner.

Just as she was pocketing a paltry sum for a favorite hair ornament of her sister's, she noticed a man watching her from across the way. Not just any man, but possibly the same who'd looked down at her from atop his horse the other day, and who she thought might be the man called Rhomer.

To her surprise, he approached and addressed her in a low voice. "Are you Rennie Tallis?"

"Yes. And you are?"

"Hans. May we speak privately?"

Hans might be his other name, or maybe just his first name, for all she knew. She hesitated at the possibility of going somewhere alone with him, before reminding herself, if this indeed was Rhomer, the loremaster had recommended him to her. "I guess," she said.

"I'll go ahead. Meet me behind Langley's Stables in five minutes." He slipped away.

A few minutes later, Rennie set off to the meeting place after asking the potter to keep an eye on her wares.

The man slouched against the back of the stables with his hat drawn down over the top of his face. He raised it when he heard her coming.

"Are you Rhomer?" Rennie asked.

"Some call me that. Around here, I'm Hans."

"I think you saw me when I was looking for you a few days ago. Why didn't you speak to me then?"

"I have to be cautious. I learned your father was head of council."

"That's true." She felt chastised. "Then why approach me now?"

"I spoke to the loremaster." His smile lit up his otherwise bland face, projecting warmth and interest. "He's a big admirer of yours."

"He's kind."

"Would you like to tell me why you were looking for me?" Hans said.

"I'm leaving Skalbourne. The loremaster told me you might have maps of the lesser known routes and trails."

"I can get those for you. Where are you headed?"

She hesitated to say what amounted to heresy, but since the loremaster had vouched for him, she plunged forward in a lowered voice. "Do you have any idea where I might find the heretics?"

His eyes narrowed as he looked at her like he was taking her measure. "They don't want to be found. They're nomads who never stay in one place for long. Why are you looking for them?"

"I want to join them."

He swatted a fly off his trousers. "Well then. You should know the heretics are most likely to be encountered in the Savagelands to the south. What's your age, by the way?"

"Seventeen," she lied, adding two years to her real age.

He looked like he didn't believe her. "You should think twice rather than leave before your Rite. I'm sure you know, if you succeed in getting away, you can't ever return here. You'll be hung for treason."

"There's nothing for me here anymore."

"You have no idea the hardships you'll encounter in the Savagelands. I doubt you can survive it."

"You know nothing about me. I'm stronger than you think."

A flicker of amusement passed over his face. "Despite the dangers, I'll consider helping you. These are unusual times. There may be good reason to leave Skalbourne sooner rather than later."

"What reason?"

"Too complicated to explain now." He glanced past her at something. "I need to go. I'll consider your request. You won't hear from me again if I decide against it."

"But I need your help *now*."

He lowered his hat on his forehead and set off without reply.

44

TOMMIS

At the sight of the cyclops, Tommis shook from head to toe. The only thing worse would've been a giant version of Pa returned from the dead. How would he defeat this monster with no defense aside from a little drink he took before starting out?

But it didn't take long before he discovered the limits of the chain that held the creature's ankles. He skirted round the opposite edge of the arena and kept out of reach.

Soon, he approached the small opening that led outside. He could glimpse the freedom of the path and the green trees that bordered it when the cyclops spoke the words that gave him pause: "Forgetting something?"

He had already slowed down before then, astonished by how easy it appeared to evade the giant. After all, the mighty Jarem had failed to complete the Trials. They had been informed of his death following sunset on the day he was sent off. Having the first two competitors die—particularly such impressive-seeming competitors—had nearly sucked away Tommis's hope of success. Since then, they'd had two winners—numbers three and five. Tommis was the seventh, so several more could still win after him. Yet the two who'd succeeded so far were not people Tommis would've picked. Number five, Sareena—the girl who'd been at their table the first day—had a certain boldness though. That might've been what carried her through.

That Jarem had died gave him a certain satisfaction, but it almost made him regret volunteering. If Ayva had not been picked to be blest, with Jarem out of the picture, he might've succeeded in wheedling his way back into her good graces.

But he was getting distracted, which was the last thing he needed. He had quickly determined that the far end of the arena was out of the giant's reach. Yet he knew in his heart he was missing something essential. He was about to find out what it was.

When the giant pulled the tarp off his unconscious mother, Tommis's stomach twisted inside him. She was such a helpless little thing, and so tiny he thought the cyclops could probably crush her with one finger.

While he looked at her, a memory came to him. He was four years old, and Pa had just whipped him on his backside with his belt till his ass was bruised and bleeding. All for the offense of his accidentally knocking over a glass and breaking it.

Winom was there. His big brother, who he barely thought about anymore because he'd been gone so long. Winom had tried to get Pa to stop, and received a hard slap across the face for his efforts. Ma had not been home, but it would've made no difference if she had.

This was the worst beating Pa had given Tommis up to that point in his life, and he nursed a deep resentment over it. A few days later, in the heat of his anger, he stole Pa's pewter cup. He knew Pa treasured the thing, the way he kept it on a special shelf. But only later did he learn that Apollo had once drunk a sip of water from it. From then on, no one was allowed to use it or even touch it. Pa worshipped on the altar of Apollo's cup. Yet Tommis didn't just steal the cup. He threw it as far as he could into the lake. Winom saw him do it but arrived too late to stop him, and no amount of diving into the water allowed him to find it.

When Pa returned from a miserable day at work, he noticed the cup missing immediately. He roared at his two sons, threatening to kill them both if neither admitted to taking it. When neither did, he snatched up Tommis and threw him against the wall.

"I did it," Winom said. He was five years older than Tommis and had a natural instinct to protect him. "I threw it in the lake. I'm sorry, Pa. I was upset when you whacked Tommis with the belt."

Winom braced himself for a beating, yet he must've believed he'd be better able to survive it than Tommis. But all of Pa's fury came out in a single blow to Winom's head, which knocked him straight into the central beam of the house. His skull fractured front and back and he died instantly. At least he didn't suffer more than a second.

Tommis told himself he would've protested Winom's confession and admitted he was the guilty one if there'd been time. But now that his brother was dead, he reasoned, what benefit would there be to telling the truth? It would only make Winom's sacrifice meaningless if both of them were killed.

When Ma came back, she was beside herself with grief. Pa would say nothing more than that it was an "Accident," so she went to Tommis for the truth. When she asked who had really stolen the cup, Tommis lied and said his brother had. But he was only four and a terrible liar, and he saw in her face she didn't believe him. She kept his secret, though. She never breathed a word to Pa. At the same time, she changed a little toward him. She continued to support him in every way she could, but there was a distance. Almost like he scared her.

Let go of sentimentality, self-blame, and assumptions based on what you've been taught. Place your trust in the immortals. He whispered Aphrodite's words to himself, as he had many times since she'd spoken to him.

The memory of Winom's death brought with it a physical sensation, like an invisible python wrapped around his head, squeezing, squeezing till it felt as if his brains would pop out. Though Pa had been the one to kill him, Tommis could never forget that Winom paid the price for his taking the cup. Living with this memory had much to do with who he'd become. Solitary, devoted to the immortals and determined to become their valued servant. He would bring honor and glory to his family name. For the first time, he understood it had been necessary for Winom to die so that he could live.

Ma, too, must be sacrificed. If he tried to rescue her, chances were good the Cyclops would kill them both, rendering all their deaths meaningless. Pa had been another whose demise had been required to ensure Tommis's ascension.

Let go... He understood this trial was not a test of his physical ability to overcome a monster. The immortals knew all of them had undergone years of physical training. The Trial was a test of mind and heart. Did he have the intelligence to recognize the easiest approach to forward movement? Did he have the strength of purpose to turn his back on his own past and his own affections in order to follow the path the immortals laid out for him? This is what he would prove by saying goodbye to his mother right here, right now. If she knew, she would approve of his decision. But it no longer mattered. He needed to break the bonds of home and family and become the master of his own fate.

He watched as an eagle circled downward from above and flew out the open doorway to freedom. Zeus was master of the eagles. He needed no other sign to ensure he was making the right choice. When the cyclops shouted, "Come back here, or watch me crush every bone in her body," he was through the door and no longer listening.

45

TOMMIS

The sirens were more beautiful than any woman Tommis could imagine, except Ayva. Their voices swirled through his head, carrying a sensation of restfulness and tranquility. In fact, he welcomed them as a distraction, to keep his thoughts from turning back to Ma, and how he had just left her behind, and the terrible death that she must have suffered.

The sirens made him want to stop right there and never finish the Trials. To remain under their loving oversight forever. But he knew from Odysseus's story they were not as they seemed. That they meant to lure him to his death.

And yet he couldn't help turning his bow in their direction and rowing harder.

Let go of sentimentality, self-blame, and assumptions based on what you've been taught. Aphrodite's words continued to run through his head. *Assumptions.* He twirled that around on his tongue.

What if this was not the same as Odysseus's story? He considered this. The way he escaped the cyclops had certainly not been the same. What would be a different way to escape the sirens, aside from rowing past them as Odysseus did? Come to think of it, he could not escape as the hero did, lashed to his mast. Tommis had no men to do the rowing.

Maybe he ought to kill them. But he had no weapons. Would they stand still while he smashed each of their heads with an oar? And what really would that get him? Possibly he'd gain the will to continue rowing in the other direction, toward where it appeared the path continued.

He paused in his rowing to stare at the sirens. Their gowns were the same hue as the immortals' markings. That they were so sheer you could see their gorgeous bodies through the fabric was a distraction, of course. The color alone signaled their connection to the immortals. He did not need another sign.

He rowed harder. After all, he only had till sunset and he had no idea how long it might take to complete the last and possibly most challenging of the trials.

When he reached shallow water, the sirens reached out for his boat and pulled it in. When he turned to face them, he discovered they had transformed into horrible creatures, half-fish, half-mortal, with terrifying claws that stretched out toward him. It was all he could do not to swim away from them.

Instead, he let them grasp his arms on both sides and lead him up onto the meadow. They screeched into his ear, the beautiful song gone. He was terrified they would put him in a pot to boil for their dinner. Despite this, he resisted trying to break away as they dragged him forward.

The path, bound by the blue rope, continued ahead. When they reached it, they let Tommis go, giving him a parting shove. He ran to keep them from grabbing him again, though he didn't hear their steps behind him. Eventually he turned back to see what they were doing, but by then they were gone.

He continued at a fast pace, fighting off the memories of Ma that threatened to derail his focus and concentration.

ONE MORE TRIAL REMAINED, and it frightened Tommis even more than the cyclops. *Scylla*, her six heads slathering at the mouth for a taste of him, whipping around on their monstrous necks. He thought where there was Scylla there must be Charybdis, but the trail to the right looked empty, as if it would be a simple matter to take that route instead.

Part of the seemingly empty route was hidden behind boulders, though. Maybe a cyclone would start up by the time he reached that section. Still, it didn't matter.

The one thing that mattered was the sign carved in stone next to Scylla: *In Immortals We Trust.*

He had no weapon, but with or without, he would've made the same choice. He must prove to the immortals he was prepared to follow them to the very depths of Hades and back by walking into that den of six slathering jaws. In truth, he trusted them, particularly Aphrodite, to protect him. Hadn't they done so up till now?

He approached Scylla. Her many faces seemed to be smiling at him in an evil way, as if to say, *we've got you now*. He might die by being torn to bits by her. Or he might survive in some manner he didn't yet understand.

In Immortals We Trust. This had to be the key. With no weapons, no way of defending himself, not even a stone or a stick, he needed to place his trust in the immortals.

Tommis moved toward the snapping heads, closed his eyes, and prayed. *Have mercy on this humble mortal whose only wish is to serve you as a defender.* The noises of the beast grew louder and more horrifying. His nose filled with her raw, rancid stench of blood and filth. Holding the rope to guide him, he took a single step forward with his entire body bracing for the attack. He still heard her movements and her screeching, but he felt nothing. He took another step, and then another. Except for the noise, it was as though she'd disappeared. He wanted to look, but feared that would ruin everything by showing a distrust in the immortals. So he kept his eyes closed and continued walking until Scylla's yowling came from behind him.

When he opened his eyes and looked back, she appeared as ferocious as ever, and yet somehow he'd walked right through her. He gave thanks to the immortals for preserving him, and did not pause to dwell on the mystery of his experience. He hurried along the trail and soon saw the end of it, where Captain Broyland and a group of defenders awaited him.

The captain clapped Tommis on the back. "Well done, son. You've won the Trials and qualified to join the ranks of the defenders."

As the rush of excitement over successfully completing the Trials began to dissipate, he couldn't help but wonder if all of it was real. Was Ma really dead? He was not likely to ever find out. Defenders were never stationed in their hometowns, and he planned to remain with them for his lifetime.

He pushed away all thoughts of Ma, Pa, Winom, and Skalbourne. A new life in service to the immortals lay ahead of him now.

PART II

EXODUS

During the Dark Age, heretics who defied immortal guidance took over the governance of Hellas. They were motivated solely by greed and the desire for power. Science was the tool they wielded to achieve their ends, with no consideration for its harmful effects on Hellenes. They nearly destroyed Hellas itself.

Heresy is the vile snake that must be stamped down whenever it raises its foul head, lest the sins of the past be repeated.

-The Book of the Immortals

46

RENNIE

On her way back from the market, Rennie mulled over what to do if Hans refused to help her. But the sight of two workers preparing the gallows for a hanging in the center of the square drew her up. She approached and stood behind two women who were talking among themselves after pausing to watch.

"Who's it for, do you think?" the younger of them asked.

"The Woodgard woman, I imagine," replied the other. "That's who I heard about. Kept her blind child, you know?"

"Ah, then, I suppose she deserves it. Who would want to keep such a child? More trouble than they're worth."

"I don't know about that."

"And what about him? Will he be hanging next to her, do you think?"

"I heard they let him go."

"No! Are you certain? Why would they?"

"He was a baby. He didn't choose to break the law. Punishment enough being blind, the immortals said."

"Ah, then, bless the immortals for their mercy."

Rennie felt terrible for Jarem's mother and wondered if

it were true his brother had been freed. Could he be back home by himself? She hoped he could manage living alone.

Moving on, she was unable to think charitable thoughts about the immortals and their so-called mercy, as she pictured her nanny's death at the base of Zeus's statue. She and Ayva had meant to visit the widowed husband and offer sympathy, but there had been no time and now her sister was gone.

She returned home at the risk of facing Poppa's wrath. It was with relief that she found their house empty again. It shamed her to think it, but her father was a coward. Fine. This would give her time to check for Xander's return and prepare for her own departure.

She searched outside without finding any evidence of the colt and tried to push him out of her mind; it wasn't as though she could actually keep a blest horse without anyone ever learning about it. Her thoughts turned to Rhomer's warning about the consequences of skipping out before her Rite. This made her hesitate regarding her next steps, though the chance of Poppa's returning within the next few days, noticing Ayva's empty room, and demanding the money from the sales was a powerful reason not to delay. If necessary, she would set out without expectation of help from Hans or anyone else.

Rennie went to her room to gather what she needed for traveling. It was difficult deciding what things might be essential, and what she could do without if she tried. Weight must be kept to a minimum to avoid sore joints and exhaustion. She would pick up an item ready to add it to her essential pile, then stare at it for a moment, thinking. Most often, she ended up setting it back down after that.

She was nearly done when she realized she hadn't checked her bedside table for anything that might be useful.

She almost turned away from it, not wanting to be tempted by something that might hold emotional value but would not be of any actual use. But she couldn't resist glancing into it, if only to hold the memory inside her head of what once was hers.

When she opened the drawer, though, she blinked several times at the object inside, wondering if she was imagining it. At first she was puzzled, because she knew it didn't belong to her, but then she drew her breath in sharply at the realization of what it was.

The gold medallion. It had to be the same as what Belic wore that night. But how did it end up here?

Her house had been searched the day after she saw Belic. She struggled to remember if she had checked this drawer then. Were there signs they had searched it? She really couldn't recall. However, she could still picture how completely they went through everything in the house. It didn't seem possible they could've missed this one drawer.

Meaning Belic had been here since then. She looked up suddenly. Could he still be here now? She went into the other rooms, checking everywhere in case he might be hiding. But he wasn't in the house, nor did she find any sign of his having been there.

She returned to her room and snatched up the medallion to scrutinize it. A tingling sensation filled her—half dread, half excitement.

It appeared to be solid gold, with a diameter of roughly an inch and a half. The thick, round object hung on a golden chain. A small blue gem that she thought might be a sapphire glittered from its center. The medallion had to be valuable, yet she could hardly sell it.

She turned it over. On the back, the metal was smooth and shiny except in the middle, where a number was etched: 8472256. That seemed odd. She had seen jewelry with a small stamp indicating the metal smith, but never a long number like this. She wondered what it could mean.

Why had Belic chosen to give it to her? She remembered his wound. Maybe he thought he would die soon. Maybe he had decided to see the doctor for treatment and feared the man would turn him in to the immortals.

Whatever the reason, she considered it a solemn trust. She lifted the chain over her head and tucked the medallion under her blouse. She would keep it close at all times and not rest until she found out its purpose, and if it might be used to bring down the dominion of the immortals.

The immortal Ares was desperately seeking this medallion. She was sure of it. A sudden weakness flowed through her limbs, making her reach out to the table to steady herself. He would boil her alive if that was what it took to get the thing back from her. If she was smart, she would head to the lake as fast as her legs could take her, and hurl the medallion into it.

Instead, she clasped her fingers around it and resolved to disappear from Skalbourne tonight.

47

RENNIE

A knock came at the door just as Rennie sat down to write a note to Poppa. Her breath caught in her throat at the possibility that it might be Ares or any of his defenders, but the voice of the loremaster's assistant coming through from outside put her fears to rest.

"It's me, Kern. Can I come in?"

She still checked the peephole to make sure he was alone before letting him in. Even then she peered past him to make sure there was no sign of Poppa, nor any immortals or defenders approaching in the distance.

After shutting the door, she greeted him. "What brings you here tonight?"

He extended his satchel to her. "The loremaster told me to bring you this. From Rhomer."

Rennie peeked into the bag and saw what looked like a map. She prickled with excitement. "Oh, thank you. Can I get you some tea or a bit of cake?"

"Um, sure."

She set the satchel inside her room in case Poppa came home, before putting the kettle on the heat. Then she cut him a generous piece of the cake she'd purchased for Poppa and placed it in front of him on the table.

After several bites, Kern said, "Do you know Jarem Woodgard has a twin brother, name of Fenn?"

"Yes, I heard about that. Why do you ask?"

"Did you know they arrested him, and then later they released him?"

"I heard something today, but I wasn't sure if it was true."

"It was. He's living all alone at their house, because, well, you probably know the mother's in jail and his brother is doing the Trials."

"He's lived there all his life," Rennie said. "I suppose he can manage by himself?"

"Sure, if that was all there was to it. But people can be cruel. They attacked him on his way home; luckily the loremaster came along and helped him. Then the other night they came to Fenn's house and painted "Defective," and threw rocks and such."

Her blood boiled to hear the way Fenn had been treated. But there wasn't anything she could do about it. "I hope he's all right." She knew her words sounded lame.

"He had the place locked up well. They didn't get in. This time."

"I'm very sorry to hear about it." She poured Kern's tea and brought it to him.

"He could really use a friend right now," the boy said.

"Is that what this is about? Did the loremaster put you up to this?"

"He and I see eye to eye on most things."

She smiled at the grownup way Kern liked to talk. "I wish I could help. Don't tell anyone, but I'll be leaving town very soon. I'm afraid you and the loremaster will need to find another friend for Fenn."

Kern finished his tea and cake quickly and went on his way. Poppa still hadn't returned, so she was pretty certain now he wouldn't be coming back tonight. This was her chance. Along with her few items of clothing and personal hygiene, she was bringing a blanket for sleeping on, a tarp in case of rain, and food and water to last her several days. She gathered everything into Poppa's backpack so she could walk with her hands free. It couldn't matter to him that she was taking it, since he hadn't used it in years.

She unrolled the new map, which showed far more detail than the one given her by the loremaster. She recognized a few of the local pathways, but others were unknown to her. And the Savagelands, which contained no detail on the other map, now showed two passages running through it, along with the depiction of several notable landmarks. She silently thanked Rhomer.

Following careful consideration, Rennie figured out the route for tonight. Her plan was to travel after dark as much as possible, particularly along the Skalbourne trails that were well-trafficked by day. Frequent travelers helped keep the paths smooth, so she wouldn't need to worry too much about tripping in the dark. Moreover, tonight was a clear night with a bright half moon. She might not get conditions as good as these for some time.

She sat down to write the note to Poppa. "I have left home so you won't have to see me anymore. First I sold Ayva's things because she won't need them and I knew she'd want me to have them. So I have some money to get started. I'll send word when I find a new place to live. In the meantime, I'm staying with a friend. Don't worry about me, I'll be fine. Love, Rennie."

She decided not to tell him where she was going in case he sent someone to find her and bring her back. He would do anything to prevent her from leaving town before next year's Rite. Therefore, it was necessary to hold back information regarding her true destination, and hope he would have little enough interest to investigate precisely where she had gone.

She was ready now. When she got outside, she again spent several minutes checking the shed and all around it for Xander's possible return. She had cried many tears over him the night before, amazed by how quickly the sweet colt had caused her to love him. It was for the best she no longer had charge of a blest horse, but it broke her heart to think he had lost his life on her watch.

Rennie tightened her shoulders and drew in a deep breath of cool air that carried the unexpected scent of wood smoke. Glancing all around, she spotted a reddish-orange glow in the distance. Something was burning.

48

FENN

The sensation of something pushing against his back woke Fenn from a heavy sleep. He exploded into a coughing fit and felt another thrust against his side. The blest colt neighed while he struggled to get his mind around what was happening.

He continued wheezing, breathing in smoke, he realized. He was burning hot like with a fever. His pajamas clung to his sweaty skin. Flames crackled. *The house is on fire.* He fumbled toward the closed door, but jerked his hand away before searing it on the knob. The fire must've started in the front part of the house. They could not escape in that direction.

The horse had been trying to wake him. "Come on, Boy. This way."

He heard the colt follow him to the window. Fenn raised it up only to realize he had nailed the bedroom shutters in place after he'd discovered sections where the wood had splintered during the last attack on his house.

He might've been able to accept his own departure from this miserable world, but not the colt's. The horse deserved a chance at life. His mind scrambled to think of something heavy inside the room that he could use to batter the shutter. He remembered the wooden chair in the corner, lifted it up, slammed it against the shutter over and over. He paused and checked the wood; it was close to breaking apart. Fenn raised the chair once more and thrust it as hard as he could.

The chair broke and fell in shambles. Fenn dropped back on the edge of the bed. His eyes filled with tears. "I'm sorry, Boy," he whispered.

He heard the horse moving. Something pounded against the shutter and then came the sound of wood cracking. Boy must've slammed his head into it and broken through. Fenn used a chair leg to break off the last bits that blocked their way.

"You go now, boy," he said.

And just like the horse could understand his every word, he must've raised up on his rear legs and pushed off of them out the window. Fenn heard him landing outside.

He hesitated. The house was going to burn down; without doubt, the fire was already too large for him to stop it. But what could he save from his room? His thoughts flew to his new cane, lying on Jarem's bed, and the chess set. The latter lay beyond his reach on the kitchen table; he'd been playing it yesterday evening. He snatched up the cane, thinking how much he would like to keep a memento that would remind him of his mother as well, but it just wasn't possible.

He tossed the cane from the window before climbing out. With one hand gripping the sill, he lowered his body and let go, rolling as he hit the ground. His landing hurt, though it didn't feel as if he broke any bones, or sprained any joints.

Fenn heard the colt trotting away. "Boy! Come back here!" he shouted.

He wondered if the people who started the fire were still here, watching him, waiting to see the blind boy stumble in the darkness. It didn't matter; nothing mattered anymore. Let them kill him and get the suffering over with. But until then, he was sticking with the colt. Feeling around on the ground, he found his cane and set off after the sounds of the horse crashing through the underbrush.

"Boy, come back!" he called again. He kept going until the noises stopped and he could no longer tell which direction he should take. Pausing, he leaned against a tree, thinking that if he had a knife, he would've slit his throat right then and there. No mother, no brother, no home, and now, not even an animal to comfort him. Mother had sacrificed her life for nothing. If only she'd allowed him to die as an infant.

"Xander!" a girl's voice cried out in the distance. "Xander, you're alive!"

Fenn's skin tingled. Was this one of his cruel attackers? But she had said *you're alive*. She must be talking to the colt, he thought. Maybe the horse had belonged to her before he'd been injured and went missing. This would explain why he'd run off; he had caught the scent of her in the air.

With nothing left to lose, he called out. "The colt was wounded. I sewed him up!"

There was silence, save for the sounds of the inferno behind him. But then approaching footsteps crunched the leaves.

"I'm Jarem Woodgard's brother," he said, trying to put her at ease. "Fenn." He prayed she wasn't anything like the ones who had been tormenting him.

All at once, a hand gripped his and pulled. "You need to

get away from here. Your house is burning down! The fire brigade is slow getting here. We might be in the path of the flames."

"Who are you?"

"Don't talk now."

He let her draw him away, and he heard the colt, who she'd called Xander, with them. Now and then she'd mutter encouragements for him to keep up. They walked for some time without speaking until she paused.

"How did the fire start?" she said.

"I don't know. Boy, I mean Xander, woke me up. He saved my life."

"Maybe you left the flame going on the stove?"

It prickled that she thought his being blind and careless was the cause. "It wasn't me. Someone set it on purpose. Some people in this town can't stand the thought of me being alive, I guess."

"Some people are shit." She made cooing sounds at the horse. "Thank you for saving Xander. I thought he was dead."

"I found him in the woods and brought him home with me. Stitched him up. I think he's fine now. Xander's his name?"

"That's right."

"What's your name?"

"I'm Rennie Tallis. My sister Ayva—"

"I know who you are. Jarem mentioned you before. Thanks for getting me away from the fire."

"What are you going to do now?" Rennie asked. "Where do you want to go?"

He had nothing to do and nowhere to go. Wasn't that obvious?

49

CHARLET

Charlet's questions to the guards went unanswered. Where was Fenn? What happened to Jarem at the Rite? She wondered too if Jarem might also be arrested, but she didn't voice that thought for fear of putting the idea into someone's head.

She knew she was going to die soon. There was no way around it. Neither mortals nor immortals would pardon her crime. No one had ever escaped punishment for an offense like hers. Soon enough they would come for her, and take her to the gallows, and that would be the end. She tried to make her peace with it. Of course, she'd known when she decided to hide Fenn that this was the likely result someday. But she hadn't thought enough about what would happen to her sons. Not just Fenn, whose life would have been forfeited anyway if she'd followed the law. Jarem could also end up paying with his life for an action that had been her choice and no one else's.

She prayed to die alone. Let them not bring either of her sons to the gallows along with her. That would be more than she could bear, seeing them in the instant before all of their deaths. She prayed and prayed they would take her and kill her alone.

Charlet didn't know how many days had passed when they came for her. She had been dozing; she never really slept in this place. The rattle of the key in the lock woke her. It was still dark, but she thought morning could not be far off. She knew this must be the end because no one had come after supper and before morning light before. The two defenders carried lanterns. They weren't prison guards, another sign that her time was up. They were going to prepare her for a dawn hanging.

"You're coming with us," one of them said.

She walked between them. There wasn't any point in asking questions or protesting, because everything was decided and nothing she said would change it. But she continued to pray to the merciless immortals that the boys would be spared.

The guardhouse felt strangely empty as they passed through it. She saw no other sentries, and they led her outside through what appeared to be a hidden gate at the rear of the building. A dark carriage lay in wait, no doubt to transport her to the gallows. A defender opened the door for her.

Only then did she raise her head and recognize Apollo seated inside. She squeezed her eyes shut, expecting him to disappear, a figment of her imagination. But when she looked again, he was still there, his expression amused. It made no sense. Why would he ride to the gallows with her? Immortals did not associate themselves with the condemned.

"My lord," she said at last, dipping her head. She didn't know what else to say to him.

"Mrs. Woodgard."

The carriage rolled forward.

"Aren't you curious about where we're going?" Apollo said.

"I assumed... aren't you taking me to the gallows?"

He laughed. "Do you think immortals ride with condemned prisoners?"

"Well no... but here you are."

"I'm taking you away from here. We're going to Hardwaite."

"Hardwaite? Will you hang me there?"

"You have hanging on the brain. No, you'll start a new life there, under a new name."

"But... why?"

"Is it so difficult for you to accept good fortune? Because I need your skills as a hunter, like I told you before. I'm going to hold you to that."

"Then why not just pardon me?"

He expelled air. "It isn't for our own sakes that we immortals must appear to uphold the law. It angers mortals when we make exceptions. We must at least appear to apply the laws uniformly."

"So instead you ignore the law in secret? I don't believe mortals would love you for that, either."

"You seem to be overlooking the fact that I'm here saving your life."

She was grateful for that. It seemed he was acting on his own, without agreement from the other immortals. Because the plan had been to bring her to Olympus, but now it was Hardwaite, a town in the north.

But they hadn't yet discussed the most important part. "What about my sons?"

His gaze shifted sideways. "They were going to arrest

Jarem. The council decided he was complicit in hiding Fenn and therefore should also be charged. But he ran away, and later, came to the Rite and volunteered for the Trials. I was presiding and I accepted his pledge. The council could do nothing about it."

Without thinking about who this was, she grasped Apollo's hand and squeezed it in grateful relief. Her blood warmed at the touch of him and she dropped his hand quickly, horrified she might convey her attraction to him. "I beg your pardon, my lord."

He blinked and moved his hand away.

"With all my heart, I thank you for saving Jarem," she said.

"He saved himself."

"And..." She could hardly breathe. "Has he undergone the Trials yet? Did he succeed?"

"I don't know. I haven't received word."

She wished she could have confirmation immediately. Yet she had faith in his abilities. He would succeed, she was sure of it. "And... what of my other son?"

"I obtained his release by arguing that being blind was sufficient punishment in itself."

A tingle of delight rushed through her. "Bless you, my lord," she murmured. It occurred to her she had never said such a thing to an immortal before.

"I'm sorry, but there's more." The solemn way in which he spoke punctured the bubble of joy that had just filled her.

"After your boy returned home, there was a fire," he said. "He didn't make it out of the house alive."

She hadn't cried in years, but now her eyes filled, and the tears spilled out onto her cheeks in a continuous flow that she was helpless to stop. Her little Fenn... her sweet, smart, lovely little Fenn who had faced his short, challenging life with unnatural bravery. His loss crushed her heart and would never allow it to heal.

She buried her face in her hands as the carriage carried her toward freedom.

50

JAREM

When Jarem finally regained consciousness, pain racked his body. At first he couldn't remember anything about what he was last doing, or why he hurt so much, but gradually the memories of the Trials returned. He recalled the path sinking beneath his feet and then being swallowed up by the sand. He couldn't have fallen too far, though, or he would be dead now.

Maybe he *was* dead, though. They'd always been told that was the only possible result for someone who didn't complete the Trials. He didn't believe that falling into a sand pit qualified as a successful completion. Maybe he was in purgatory now. A waiting stop before they would transport him to Hades.

He wondered why he still ached so much if he was dead. Whatever he was lying on wasn't helping; it felt like a slab of cold, hard stone. He wished he could see better. The room was pitch dark and deathly silent.

With difficulty, he pulled himself into a sitting position.

THE TRIALS

His stomach heaved and he retched on the floor. Dizziness overwhelmed him, and he lowered his head toward his knees.

A door swung open and a loud voice shouted: "Get up, you lazy fuck!"

The man raised a lantern in one hand and held a forked stick in the other. He had patches of red skin on his face and bare head, and he was bent over in a strange way. Jarem realized with a shock the man's back was thick and misshapen.

The man jabbed him in the ribs. "Get up, I said!"

Jarem rose as quickly as he could to avoid another jab. "Who are you?" he said.

"Your worst nightmare. Benfry's the name. Move! Out the door!"

Jarem staggered to the outside, where the horizon was just beginning to light up. All around were dismal shacks, like the one he'd just come out of, perched on a bleak mountain ledge. Miserable-looking men and women streamed out from the buildings, prodded by more handlers like Benfry.

Everyone was moving in the same direction, toward the gaping dark mouth of a cave that opened up in the side of the mountain.

"What is this place?" Jarem asked.

"Hades." Benfry laughed.

Jarem could almost believe it. So much so that he wasn't even very surprised when he spotted Kailo, the first of the twelve to undergo the Trials, who was also supposed to be dead.

He maneuvered to Kailo's side. "Are we dead?" he asked in a low voice.

Kailo raised an eyebrow on seeing him, but expressed no further surprise. "Seems like it."

"Where are we going?"

"You'll see soon enough."

Benfry shoved Jarem from behind. "Get moving! No talking!"

The mass of people, with Jarem pressed into the center, flowed into the mountain. When he passed through the entrance, the movement slowed and he blinked up at the enormous cavern, with lanterns strewn across the outer walls for lighting.

A young woman, perhaps no more than fifteen, slumped next to him, her expression weary and resigned.

"What is this place?" he whispered.

She appeared not to hear him. He tapped her shoulder and repeated the question. She pointed at her ear and shrugged before turning away.

Jarem stared in disbelief. It seemed she was telling him she was deaf. *Defective.* Immortals didn't allow the deaf to live beyond infancy. Her parents must've hidden her like his mother did with Fenn. The girl must've been discovered and sent here.

This had to be the place of the dead. Everyone here was *supposed* to be dead.

Before long, he reached the head of the line, where people were being loaded into carts. The carts, when filled, moved off along a system of rails.

When it was his turn to get on, he tried for information one more time. "What is this place?" he asked the cart operator.

"These are the mines, son. You have to work them."

"So we're not dead?"

"Soon enough, you'll wish you were."

This had to be within the Savagelands, he thought. He knew nothing about what was to be found within the vast region, nor had he ever met anyone with that knowledge. All he had ever heard was that those who crossed the border into the Savagelands never came back.

51

TOMMIS

Tommis had not expected his first exercise as a defender to involve riding a horse. He'd never even been near one in his life. But when his commander asked if he knew how to ride, he said *yes* only because all the others did, and he didn't want to stand out as someone whose training was lacking.

When he led Leef out of the stable, the horse broke out of his grip and ran off into the corral.

Sareena, another of their group who had won the Trials, rode up behind him. "First time with a horse, eh?"

"No, I—"

"C'mon, it's obvious. Here, I'll help you. Did you greet him yet?"

"Greet?"

"Sure," she said. "You wouldn't jump on top of a person without saying hello first, would you?" She dismounted from her own horse and tied it to a post. "I'll show you."

He followed her to where Leef was chewing on grass. "Approach him slowly holding out your hand."

Tommis extended his palm facing upward.

"No, he'll think you're trying to grab him. Hold your hand facing down. Then let him sniff it."

Tommis did as she suggested, but Leef ignored him. "He's not interested."

"Damn, you're impatient. Give him time."

After another moment, Leef raised his head and sniffed Tommis's hand.

"What now?" Tommis said.

"Wait till he's done."

Leef touched his nose to Tommis's hand before moving his head away.

"It's all right now," Sareena said. "Go ahead and pet him."

Tommis smoothed Leef's side and the horse didn't object. "Should I get on him now?"

"My, aren't we in a hurry? You'll have to repeat this every day for a week first."

"Everyone else is on their horse!"

"I'm kidding! I'll show you how to mount." She lowered her voice. "What did you think of the Trials?"

"We're not supposed to talk about it." Despite that she had been helping him, Tommis wasn't at all sure he even liked Sareena. She had a tendency to want to explain everything to everyone, as if she was the master of all skills. At the same time, she made light of subjects that Tommis believed should be taken much more seriously.

"Of course we're not supposed to talk about it," she went on. "I just thought they were interesting. Simple, really. A test of loyalty, that's all."

He wondered if she had also left a mother or father or a sister or brother to die at the hands of a cyclops. If so, it amazed him she could treat it so lightly.

She whispered, "Do you think it was all in our heads? That potion they gave us to drink at the start, you know…"

"Everyone, line up on your horses!" the commander shouted.

"Oops, you better get mounted." She grasped Leef's bridle and held him steady.

Tommis couldn't help being annoyed that apparently *she* didn't have to greet the horse first.

"Left foot here and lift your right over the saddle," she said.

With her guidance, he got on the horse without overly upsetting him.

"Good luck," she said. "You've heard the rumors, right?"

"Rumors?"

"War is brewing. The immortals mean to crush out the heretics once and for all."

"Aren't they hiding in the Savagelands?"

She shrugged. "I guess." Without waiting, she set off to retrieve her own horse, leaving him to fend for himself. When no amount of urging would get Leef to move forward, another initiate was sent over to help him.

Tommis paid little attention. So far, he despised training. Why must he learn how to ride? He would need to be on the ground to slice up as many heretics as possible with his sword. Though the specter of the Savagelands sent a chill through his heart, he relished the thought of proving his merit in battle. The war could not come soon enough.

52

AYVA

Ayva was a young child lying sick in bed. Rennie was in the room, paying no attention to her. She insisted on playing with a cat on the floor right by the bed, and the cat kept meowing in a loud, annoying way that was upsetting Ayva.

"Where's Mommy?" she asked, and then her mother appeared and looked down at her with concern. "It hurts, Mommy."

Her mother raised her shirt and when Ayva looked down at herself, she saw a rat gnawing on her chest. In the dream, she screamed. But she must not have actually screamed because she woke right after that and the room was quiet except for Blest Iris leaning over her and whispering, "Blest Raven."

She felt hot, like she might have a fever, and her breast throbbed from the heat and pain of the branding that was recently applied. At first she thought Blest Iris must have come to give her medicine and make her feel better. Morning had not yet broken. The room was still dark and she could hear the breathing of Katreen—*Blest Crystal*—in the small bed beside her.

"You need to get dressed," Blest Iris hissed.

All she wanted to do was lie there and have someone take care of her. She closed her eyes again.

"Raven, you have to get up." Blest Iris shook her arm.

Ayva looked at her. "Why must I?"

"Get up. Here are your clothes." Blest Iris set the clothes on the bed before lifting her into a sitting position.

Though her head was fuzzy from sleep and possibly a fever, Ayva unlaced her nightgown. "Are we going somewhere?" she asked.

"Not me. You."

"I don't understand. Where am I going?" Ayva said, while Blest Iris helped lift the gown over her head.

"I don't know."

"But my training isn't done, is it?"

"When an immortal sends for you, you go. You don't argue," Blest Iris said.

Ayva looked across at Katreen, who shifted and resumed her light snoring. "Isn't she coming?"

"It's just you."

Ayva pulled on her underclothes and blouse with the help of Blest Iris. "But who sent for me? How does anyone there even know me?"

When Blest Iris didn't answer, Ayva thought of Moros, who had always been kind to her and had often complimented her on her demeanor.

"Is it Moros? Would he like me to be his handmaiden?" A hopeful spark lit up inside her. She could almost be happy waiting on Moros. She knew him already and felt comfortable in his presence. He would be a considerate master, she thought.

"It isn't Moros." Blest Iris helped her with the skirt.

"Who else then—?" Ayva suppressed a gasp at the image that came into her mind. Ares, who had stared in her direction when she got out to see what had happened on the road.

"Let's do the buttons on your skirt," Blest Iris said.

"Is it..." Ayva hardly dared say it. "Is it Ares?"

She heard Blest Iris catch her breath and knew it must be true. Silently, she cursed herself for getting out of the carriage. If only she had stayed where she was. He never would've seen her. She would've been safe.

"I can't... he's a monster," she whispered.

"Shhh. Never, ever say such a thing."

"I beg you, don't make me go."

"It isn't in my power to stop them from taking you."

Ayva pulled on her shoes. "Where are they? Out front?"

"You can't escape them," Blest Iris said.

Despite feeling weak and dizzy when she stood up, Ayva rushed to the door and peered out. The corridor was empty.

"Come with me," Blest Iris said.

Ayva turned down the hall in the direction that she thought led to the back of the fortress, and ran.

"Stop!" a man called out. Footsteps slapped the floor behind her. Before she could reach the stairs, she was grasped on both sides.

"Let me go!" she cried.

They held her tight and carried her away.

53

CHARLET

When Charlet's grief had finished pouring out, a furious dark cloud expanded to replace it. She struggled to sit across from Apollo and appear as if she were grateful for all his efforts.

In her mind, he was still the same as all the other immortals. Unless he went into open rebellion against their tyranny, he would always be the same as them. Together, they wrote the laws that oppressed mortals, and then they made certain those laws were enforced.

Because of them, she'd had to hide the very existence of one of her sons. Because of them, he'd never had a chance of leading a normal life, or at least as normal as any other mortal was allowed to live. Because of them, he had been hauled away to prison after being discovered. Because of them, he had been subject to the universal disgust and hatred mortals were trained to feel toward defectives. Because of them, her son had suffered a torturous death, dying in the flames that engulfed his one place of refuge. She knew, of course, that he didn't start that fire himself.

Because of them, her son Fenn was dead. And by now,

her son Jarem was conscripted into their service. From the deepest fiber of her being, she abhorred every immortal. The more she thought about it, the hotter her rage burned. The windows were closed and the carriage was stifling. She strained for breath.

Apollo across from her had closed his eyes and appeared to be dozing. She looked outside, wondering what would happen if she opened the door and jumped while the carriage was moving.

She would probably break an ankle and then when they came back for her, she wouldn't be able to run away.

Using her sleeve, she did her best to wipe the sweat from her brow. At least, after all the crying, he shouldn't be surprised that her face was a mess. "Excuse me, my lord," she said.

He opened his eyes. "Yes?"

It took all her reserve to keep her voice steady. "I'm sorry to bring up such a mundane matter, but I desperately need to relieve myself."

Apollo knocked on the window looking out toward the coach driver. The man slid it open.

"How long to the next village?" Apollo asked.

"Ten minutes, my lord."

"You'll find comfortable facilities there," the immortal told her.

"I'm so sorry, but I really can't wait," she said. "I couldn't forgive myself if I accidentally soiled your beautiful carriage cushions."

"Fine." He sounded annoyed. Of course, any other mortal woman would have her private parts sewn shut rather than inconvenience an immortal.

"Driver, pull over to the side," Apollo said.

"Right away, my lord."

The horses slowed the vehicle to a stop.

Charlet forced herself to thank Apollo before she got out. She kept her face lowered to keep him from reading the determination in her eyes.

Fortunately, she'd had so little to drink in prison, she didn't need to pee at all. But assuming they were watching, she set out as if in search of a private tree to go behind. At the same time, she was madly deciding her strategy.

She could not return to Skalbourne, where if she were found, she would be executed. She could not go to any of the northern towns, where it would be too easy for Apollo to find her again. Her only chance lay in escaping to the one place that even the immortals appeared to have forsaken. The Savagelands. As soon as she put a little distance between herself and the carriage, she would head south.

Since the time when she was a little girl being taught how to hunt by her father, she had learned to move through the forest with stealth and ease. She could run like the wind, she knew what plants to use to cover her scent, she could hunt using nature's tools.

If they didn't capture her immediately, she would at least enjoy the satisfaction of having disappeared out from under the mighty all-seeing immortal's nose.

54

RENNIE

"Do you think the loremaster and Kern might have a place for me to stay?" Fenn said.

"Uh, maybe." Rennie didn't relish turning back to the library. They had made progress along the southward trail. The fire, in fact, had been good luck for them because it seemed to have drawn everyone away from this part of the forest. So far they had not had to do any quick ducking behind trees. In any case, she had tied a bandanna around Xander's forehead to hide his horn stub. She didn't think his size would give away that he was a blest horse; people would simply assume he was older than he was.

"Is the library where you want to go?" she said.

"I don't know. I don't know anybody else. And they've been kind to me."

"That's not the best reason. What would you do at the library? You can't see the pages to read."

His face pinched up in annoyance. "No kidding."

"What sorts of things can you do?" she said.

"I can beat you at chess."

"How do you know? I might be the best player in Skalbourne." She had no idea how to even move the pieces.

"I just meant I'm very good. Maybe you are too."

"No, I was kidding."

"I can skin animals," he said.

"Maybe the butcher would take you on."

"Do you think he'd let me live with him? You know I no longer have a house."

"I doubt it. He has seven kids already."

"Shit."

She glanced back to see Fenn on the ground. This was the third time he had tripped. He clearly wasn't used to walking on unfamiliar terrain with a cane.

"Sorry," he said. "I'm slowing you down."

She gave him a hand up. "We need to decide where you're going before we walk any farther."

"Well where are *you* going?"

She hesitated to tell him. He could be caught, and the truth forced out of him.

"You can trust me. I won't tell anyone," he said like he read her mind.

"I'm running away." That much was obvious anyway. "Leaving Skalbourne and never coming back."

"Why?"

"They took my sister to be blest. My father doesn't like me. There's nothing for me here anymore."

"So you have no plan?" he said. "No particular place you want to go."

"That's not quite true. I'm looking for other people like me."

"Like you? In what way?"

She was tired and decided it would be best to just get

things out in the open. "People who hate the immortals and everything they represent."

"Ah. I see."

"No, you don't see."

"Starting in on the blind jokes, are we?"

"Sorry," she said.

Fenn laughed. "Jarem had a million of them."

"So what do you think?"

"About hating the immortals and everything they represent? Fuck yeah. I'm a defective. They've given us no reason to love them."

"Glad you understand."

"I'd like to come with you."

She paused and leaned against Xander, petting him. He pressed his head against her. A moment later, she pulled a rope out of her pack and made a halter for the horse. She took another section of rope and tied that to the halter.

"I get it," Fenn went on. "I'll slow you down. And I'll draw too much of the wrong kind of attention."

"Hang onto this. I think it'll be easier if you let Xander guide you." She handed him the line.

"I'm traveling with a blest colt," she said. "You know it's a death sentence if mortals touch them? Now I'm with a defective too... well, that's just butter on the bread. Fuck them, Fenn. Are you in or out?"

55

I, ASTERIOS

Apollo was sparing no time or expense in planning a magnificent ceremony to honor Helena. As he had promised, I was slated to head the procession. A tailor had even come to take my measurements. The finest silks, the most vibrant colors, and the most sparkling jewels were all being incorporated into my raiment.

The irony of waiting years for grateful recognition of my decades of service to the immortals, only to have to skip out on it, was not wasted on me.

But the living must always come before the dead. There was nothing further I could do for my daughter. Yet my efforts could mean the difference between life and death for the foal. If Helena could speak to me now, she would have just one thing to say. *What are you waiting for?*

I wanted to leave immediately, but during daylight there was too much chance of my being spotted and thwarted. Though my grandchild was in danger of starving to death, I would have to wait till nightfall.

Since the day I destroyed my own stall, I had been sleeping in Helena's. The stable master came by after dark and made sure its gate was unlatched and left open a crack. I was sure he did not want me tearing apart another section of the stable.

I drank fully from the trough before setting out in complete darkness. Having travelled the route to Skalbourne many times with Moros in the past, I could've found my way blindfolded. But I walked a measured pace as quietly as I could manage. This enabled me to hear when travelers approached and gave me time to hide myself beside the road. A blest horse traveling without an immortal would be a strange sight indeed.

It was still night when I reached the Skalbourne stable used for housing us during visits from the immortals. Thankfully, we'd had no rain since before Helena was attacked, allowing me to pick up her scent, and to follow it to the scene of her death.

The ground was still stained with her blood. It made me weak smelling it, imagining her terror as the king eagle circled above her. She would've had no thought for herself, only her foal. I believed she must have given birth just before the attack. Otherwise, if the foal had been inside her, it would almost certainly have been killed.

The blood and afterbirth would've excited the deadly eagle into a frenzy. Helena would've been weak, unable to fully defend herself and her foal. The king eagle would likely have ignored the newborn, mostly skin and bones, in favor of the afterbirth and parts of Helena's full, bloody flank.

If only I had been there to protect her. I would've fought to the death against that foul beast. To protect Helena. To protect my grandchild.

I rallied myself. Time was wasting. The foal could be out there, alive. I owed it to Helena to find it.

I sniffed in a circle around where she had lain, searching for the foal's scent. When I found it, my heart leapt for joy. Moving outward, I was able to follow it to a clump of bushes next to a large tree. There were a few broken branches like the foal had pushed its way underneath to a little hollow beyond. I discovered several crushed blackberries on the ground. It seemed the foal had been eating them.

Here at last was proof that her child had been born. And the scent told me one more thing—the foal was male. I was grandfather to a colt.

However, as I sniffed further, I encountered a fresh odor mixed in with that of the colt. *A female mortal.* Mortals' scent differed from that of the immortals.

I stiffened. Had a mortal stolen my colt? *How dare she?* The immortals would smote her for such an offense. I would run her through with my horn when I got the chance.

Yet if this mortal had fed my foal... if she was the reason the colt was still alive... I might have to find it in my heart to forgive.

I tried to follow the trail from where mortal and foal came together. But before long, at a place where they must have gone off the main path to hide themselves, I lost their scents. I spent the rest of the night walking in circles, trying to regain them, without luck.

As the sun began to rise, I realized I was hungry and thirsty. I followed my nose to a patch of tasty greens by the side of a creek.

While I stood there growing sleepy, I experienced a sensation I had never felt before. I thought it must be *loneliness.* My mate was long gone, my daughter newly dead, and my grandchild missing. I even missed Moros. I had been his close companion all my life, and now they had taken him from me.

It took these thoughts to make the spirit inside me stir. I was a blest horse, dammit. We were a proud, if subjugated race. The immortals had abandoned me. Zeus himself was responsible for the death of my daughter, and possibly my grandchild as well. I owed them nothing. If anything, they owed me freedom in the last years of my life. I had a purpose now, to follow his scent wherever it took me, even if that was deep inside the remote lands to the south. I vowed to find the colt or die trying.

THE END

DREADMARROW
BOOK ONE OF THE THIEVES OF MAGIC
(PREVIEW)

Today, my fifth time as a russet sparrow, I felt as if I'd been flying all my life. I left caution behind, soaring over the town square, catching a beakful of rancid smoke rising from the shops and ramshackle homes. My wings flapped according to instinct and carried me toward Sorrenwood's outer edge, over rows of broken shelters. I continued across a field dotted with bent farmhands, past a thicket of trees that gave way to the swimming hole.

I flew lower to watch the three bare-chested boys who approached the water. I'd seen them before but they were younger than me and I could not remember their names. The dark one swung out on the rope and when he reached the highest point, he released with a shout and a splash. His friends followed in rapid succession, nearly landing on him. Their joy was infectious. I sailed up higher and dove down, letting myself fall until—an inch above the water's surface—I pulled up. The pale boy saw me and looked puzzled. He had probably never seen a bird play before.

I rose higher for my second dive. But as I shifted downward, a huge silhouette appeared above me... *a hawk*, its wings spread wide, a monstrous beast to sparrow-me. Shaking, I dodged left and then right and then back again, hoping to confuse it with my odd movements. I followed an erratic course and didn't realize until it was too late, that I'd crossed over the outer wall and now flew above the Cursed Wood. Gray mist seeped upwards like steam from a giant cauldron. The tips of black tangled branches reached toward me, but I knew better than to land on any of its foul trees.

The air whooshed as the hawk dove for me, and I felt a stinging sensation as it clipped off a wad of my feathers. I beat my wings in a panic, angling toward Fellstone Castle. It was a dreary, forbidding fortress but the only place I might find refuge. A shadow formed over me as the hawk prepared to dive again. My confidence shaken, I swore at myself for having so little practice flying. Whether to flap my wings or coast on the wind—I had no idea which would get me to the castle quicker. And so I flapped and coasted and flapped again, aiming to reach the nearest tower. The hawk's breath grazed my back as I flew over the moat, ducked under the edge of the roof, and hurled myself into a tight corner, where I crouched, trembling and desperately wondering what defense I could use if my attacker crawled in after me.

The hawk didn't come. Yet I feared it might still be out there, perched on the roof, waiting with uncanny stillness for me to emerge. That didn't sound like normal hawk behavior, but I knew so little about them. By now I should've been an expert on any animal that wished to make me its supper. I'd grown careless, caught up in the novelty and excitement of flying. My first time out, I only hopped across the yard and took a short flight up into the nearest tree, growing accustomed to the odd sensation of seeing things behind me. With each day I flew, I grew bolder. I'd half-believed, half-hoped the magic lent me a kind of protective shield, keeping other animals from perceiving me. I knew better now. In future, I would watch for shadows, and feel for subtle shifts in the air that flowed around me.

Movement below caught my eye. Down on the castle lawn, six armed boarmen huddled together, speaking amongst themselves in snorts and grunts. Their pig heads with sharpened tusks were disturbing enough at the best of times, combined with the bodies of herculean men, broadened by thick padding covered in chain mail. Here, alone and unprotected at the castle, I shivered in dread, and shrank further into my corner. Their leader glanced upwards, revealing heavy scars across his eyes and snout. Even from this distance, or maybe because I knew the way they always looked at you, I felt the chill of his cold, black piggish eyes, devoid of feeling. Of course he wasn't looking at me, a little bird under the roof, but at an open window below me. Seconds later, a man extended his arm out the window and lowered it in signal.

The scarred boarman bellowed at another whose ear had been partly chewed off. The group opened up, revealing a frail man on his knees at their center, his hands tied behind his back. Pale and filthy with his clothing torn into strips, he looked as if they'd dragged him from the dungeon only moments earlier. Two of the boarmen lifted him to his feet and shoved him in the direction of the forest. His poor legs appeared weak and spindly from long disuse, but still he loped toward the trees, driven by a final, desperate hope that defied all logic. *If only I could help him.* But even if I flew down to lend him my wings, by the time I changed back, and before I could show the man what to do, the boarmen would surely have murdered us both.

Run, I silently urged. *Run as if the world were on fire beneath your feet.*

The boarmen salivated and raised their spears on their leader's command. The man stumbled just before reaching the trees, clawing his way up, fighting his way forward. *Faster! Don't give up!* The leader signaled for the boarmen to unleash their blood lust, and they pummeled each other to be first to their prey. They thundered across the field, hunched over and pig-like despite having the bodies of men. Their high-pitched squeals formed a grating war cry as they crashed through the bramble into the woods. Seconds later came a heartrending shriek that froze my blood. The trees shook during the killing frenzy that must have followed.

I couldn't bear to watch any longer. I set out from my refuge, meaning to fly directly home, but instead, curiosity drew me to the window below. I had to see with my own eyes the devil who had ordered that brutal execution. Landing on the sill in the corner, I told myself there was no danger because I looked like nothing but a harmless little bird. At worst he might swish me away, and I would fly off before his hand could touch me.

The man was Lord Fellstone himself. Stripped to the waist, he sprawled in a chair by the window, his feet propped on a low table, and his hands overloaded with jeweled rings. He looked as he had when I last saw him at the Midsummer celebration, with a mane of auburn hair that, considering his age, ought to be showing some grey. His nose was sharp, his eyes shrewd, his manner bored.

But it was the tall young woman beside him who drew my eye with her extraordinary appearance. She was dressed like a man, in close-fitting apparel sewn of dark green leather. She wore a cloth cowl of the same color round her head and neck, hiding her hair. A thin leather mask covered her forehead, cheeks, and the top of her nose, leaving open her mouth and chin. This woman hunched over Lord Fellstone, holding a sturdy, intricately carved wand of black wood. Its tip caught a beam of sunlight from the window and diffused it into a wide circle over a pustulent boil on Lord Fellstone's shoulder. The infection gradually cleared until it was gone. She moved the wand over a second boil that sprawled in a circle of virulent red near his waist.

His lordship raised his head and gave me such a piercing look, it caused the contents of my stomach to flip. His eyes widened in astonishment, until a loud, "Ha!" burst from him.

The woman paused. "My lord?" She followed his gaze to sparrow-me. I tried to leap into the air and fly away, but somehow I couldn't get my claws to let go of the sill. I didn't know if I was frozen in panic or rooted in place by a silent spell Lord Fellstone cast on me.

"Oh, I do love sparrows," he said. He leaned forward, his face growing animated. "You know, this one would make a splendid appetizer for my supper tonight."

"Boiled or roasted?" said the woman.

"Cooked over an open flame on a skewer, I should say. Fetch me my sword."

I couldn't believe my ears. No sensible person would ever eat a sparrow. For two tiny bites of stringy meat, it would not be worth all the trouble of plucking. *Is his lordship mad?* I strained to pull my feet away, while they stubbornly clung to the sill.

The woman lay down the wand and retrieved a sword with jewels encrusted on its handle.

"There won't be anything left of it after we spear it with

that," Lord Fellstone said, making me wonder if he'd been playing with me all along. "Why is this bird still here anyway?" His lips curled into a smile that was ripe with evil intent.

My claws released and I shot up into the sky. I raced across the Cursed Wood and over the castle wall with one goal driving me: *get home.* Once during the flight, a shadow moved over me, but it was only a crow. As I reached the house and swooped down toward my window, the crow circled above and turned back the way we'd come. *Did the bird follow me?* I dismissed the thought as quickly as it occurred. My nerves were frayed; soon I'd be imagining eyes peering out of every tree.

The instant I touched my bedroom floor, I scraped three times with my claw. The familiar tingling sensation shot through me as I changed back into myself, Tessa Skye, sixteen years old, wearing a plain wool gown that laced up the front over my white shift. My key pouch hung from a belt that cinched my waist. It was odd how anything I wore or held onto when I changed into a bird would still be with me when I changed back, but magic was a powerful force beyond my understanding, and sometimes one had to simply accept what was, without being able to explain it.

I remained frozen for a moment, struck by the memory of that terrible hunt on the castle grounds. The shrill cry of the wretched man echoed still inside my head.

"Tessa."

I jumped and spun around at the sound of Papa's voice. He stood just behind me, framed by the doorway.

"Papa?" I said, giving him a blank look, masking my fear of what he might have seen.

His form seemed more gaunt than usual, his features stern and angular, his cheeks darkened with the stubble of three days' growth. His eyes fixed on the sparrow amulet that hung from my neck. Normally I tucked it out of sight under my gown, but I hadn't had time.

"Where did you get that?" he said.

I felt my face flush red, but I rallied, affecting a light tone. "I thought you'd gone out."

"The windrider," he said. "Tell me where it came from."

"The what?"

"Your amulet."

I hesitated before answering. "I found it."

"Where?"

"I don't recall."

"Don't tell me a falsehood. I know it was your mother's."

I wanted to bolt but he filled the doorway and I would never make it past him. "I remember now. She gave it to me," I said.

"No, she didn't," he said.

"How do you know?" A tinge of defiance crept into my voice.

"You were only four when she went away."

The old feelings of hurt and abandon rose. "I suppose she didn't love me enough to give me anything."

Papa scowled. "Don't talk nonsense. Tell me the truth. How did you get it?"

"I found it on her bedroom floor, the day she left," I said at last. "Was it so awful to take something that reminded me of her?"

"It's not a memento, it's a rare item of powerful magic. Give it to me."

I shrank back from him and clutched my throat. "No, Papa!" He had no idea what he was asking.

"You heard me. Magic is dangerous. Only the conjurers

are allowed to use it. If it were up to me, it would be banished altogether."

"But you don't know... you've never felt... there's nothing else like it. Flying is pure and it makes me feel free, and.... How could anything be wrong with it?"

"You can be sure there's a price to be paid in using that magic. Not knowing what that price is makes it all the more troubling." He reached out his hand. "You're young yet. Be patient and good things will come, but not this way."

My eyes filled with tears as I lifted the necklace over my head and handed it to Papa. "I meant no harm."

He softened at the sight of my tears and clasped me to him. "Of course not. You didn't know the danger. Now you do. We'll speak no more of it." He held me for a moment. "Have you been to the Kettlemore's yet? We can't afford to scorn paid work."

I forced my gaze from the hand that clutched my sparrow. "Yes, Papa."

He had called it a windrider. The name suited my amulet; I would use it from now on. I would not despair of flying again, as I had my ways of bending Papa to my will over time. He simply didn't understand and I must find a way to convince him of the benefits. Perhaps he could be made to grasp its value by trying it himself. He would not want to, of course. And the truth was... I didn't want to let him use it. *It's mine and I should not have to share it.*

End of preview.
Please visit margiebenedict.com for purchase options.

ACKNOWLEDGMENTS

I give thanks to all the indie authors who share their experiences in the hope of lifting us all.

I give thanks to the Scituate Senior Center, the Seaside Book Club, Leslie Andresen, Joyce Friedman, Karen Campbell, and Denise Price for their kind support.

I give thanks to these wonderful bookstores in Massachusetts for their support of local independent authors:

Storybook Cove, Hanover
Barnes & Noble, Hingham
Buttonwood Books and Toys, Cohasset
Ocean Village Bookstore, Marshfield
Book Love, Plymouth

I give thanks, as always, to my beloved readers: Tanner Kaptanoglu, Kay Liscomb, Karla Sheridan, and Sheri Davenport.

I give deepest thanks, for the first time, to Brian Hupp, my new partner in love and life, for his expertise and encouragement, and for the myriad of ways he supports me.

ALSO BY MARGIE BENEDICT

DREADMARROW (The Thieves of Magic Book One)

GRAVENWOOD (The Thieves of Magic Book Two)

KINGSHACKLE (The Thieves of Magic Book Three)

THE THIEVES OF MAGIC TRILOGY

BEFORE THE KILLING (The BEFORE Series Book One)

BEFORE SHE WAS TAKEN (The BEFORE Series Book Two)

BEFORE HE VANISHED (The BEFORE Series Book Three)

BEFORE BOOKS 1-3

INVADER

BLOOD AND VEIL

LAST GIRL STANDING

ABOUT THE AUTHOR

Margie Benedict is the author of ten published novels in the genres of science fiction, fantasy, and thriller. These include the THIEVES OF MAGIC trilogy, the BEFORE Series of time travel mysteries, and several standalone novels. Her most recent novel, THE TRIALS, kicks off a new dystopian fantasy series called ORIGINAL GODS.

Margie earned a B.A. in English from Stanford University. In addition to her novels, she has written five produced screenplays. Her script, DEAD IN THE ROOM, was made into an award-winning film starring Patrick J. Adams (of the TV show SUITS fame). In her prior career, she was a software engineer who worked at Apple Computer and designed the text-editing software for early versions of the Macintosh.

BEFORE THE KILLING is set in a fictional town similar to the one in Massachusetts where Margie grew up. She now lives there by the sea with her husband Brian and Australian shepherd Winston.

Made in the USA
Middletown, DE
08 January 2025